# DIAMOND

## for a

## RUBY

M16
SPY THRILLER

M16
SPY THRILLER

M16
SPY THRILLER

# STEFAN NICHOLSON

"To the men and women who protect our way of life - by risking their own"

Other relevant books by
**Stefan A. Nicholson**

'SAN Language Book of Instruction'

'Business Analysis Package'

'Peripheral Lives'

'Blind Familiarity'

'Symbolic Art Notation'

'JEMMA short stories'

'CIRCLE in a SPIRAL'

'SPY within a RUBY'

'DIAMOND for a RUBY'

Book three in the trilogy is: "RUBY's Covert MISSION"

There is also an original music CD – 'Pictures of Life'

*"Lest we forget . . . our inaction on homelessness, poverty and inequality."*

~ Stefan Nicholson

DIAMOND for a RUBY          First Edition August 2018

Copyright © 2018 Stefan Andrew Nicholson, Hobart Tasmania

All rights reserved

Printed in Australia

ISBN: 978-0-6482953-3-4

Published by:

ENVIROSUPPORT

P.O. Box 370, South Hobart,

Tasmania, Australia 7004

ISBN: 978-0-6482953-3-4

Website:   www.stefannicholson.com

email:      stefannicholson@bigpond.com

phone:      +61 417 181 077

# CONTENTS

# Entanglement

The early morning vigil precipitated the same deep feelings of sadness as it did every month but it was a necessary part of her healing process to remember this close friend. He had given his life whilst protecting her.

Ruby crouched down to leave the usual offering of blue woodland flowers, feeling the gaze of the cold headstone. She started weeping uncontrollably once more. Her long brown hair shielded the pain on her face like a protective curtain.

A stray cat had stopped abruptly from its dash amongst the long shadows, surprised by her sudden movement. It ran off quickly, in pursuit of its quarry arousing Ruby's senses, but she was too tired to worry. Then, she felt that same chill.

It unnerved her enough to stand up. Somebody was watching her. It was time for her to go. Whether it was real or imagined, thoughts of developing deeper emotional problems compounded her feelings of guilt.

She had not slept well at all, for the lonely week without Eric had forced her to focus on the looming anxiety for the day ahead. She was not prepared to confront those past events in public today. It was going to be agonisingly difficult.

A planned intrusion into her private grieving in the form of a get-together by friends of the deceased had arrived . . . but they were no friends of hers. Ruby had been hesitant about attending the function at the Morpeth Arms for some time. Thoughtless comments from her new work colleagues indicated that it was gearing up to be just another evening of excessive drinking, interspersed with tall stories and crass networking banter.

This after-work booze-up was certainly not her idea of remembering her much-loved mentor, Roger Davis. They would be watching her for signs of weakness. The event location was also a sticking point, located just across the river from Vauxhall Cross, home to the British Secret Intelligence Service known as MI6. It was somehow too close.

Davis often had a few drinks there, probably staring out at the fortress building and wondering what life would have been like on the 'outside', but he had long resigned himself to thinking that there was no going back. The solution was simple. He just quietly endured the continuous struggles of working on the never-ending covert assignments.

Dark thoughts about the future had consumed his every waking moment for he could no longer be an optimist. He had obtained a secret list of double agents who had infiltrated his organisation . . . but he didn't know who he could trust with its contents. Now three years since his murder, he was just another public servant in the minds of those who thought they knew him and a closed file in the classified annals of expired and retired British agents.

"Had he not given his life for his country?" she thought.

If the 'company' seemed uncaring and forgetful in its duty to the survivors of its fallen, then the neglect was mitigated by the camaraderie of his close team of field intelligence operators. They were the invisible front line chosen for their special skills. Of course, there was still the influence of class, old school and titled heritage, which enabled some mediocre recruits to rise above their abilities. It was only the upper echelon, who still cared about such tired but quietly closeted values, which intertwined around archaic policies and procedures, developed over a disturbing period of British history.

Davis had succeeded without any of these attributes. He knew better than to acknowledge that he was their best operative. Begrudgingly they had allowed him to progress 'above his station' . . . but only within his work.

Ruby was now a part of that elite fortress of knowledge and enforcement after finishing her degree with majors in Forensic Analysis and Foreign Affairs. At least, she was on probation as a potential field intelligence officer after enduring the endless sessions of background checking and psychological appraisal. She was in two minds about her tall, lithe figure, which stood out during physical training classes along with her remarkable beauty, long brown hair and social dynamism. Amorous close encounters and the inevitable innuendo were soon skilfully despatched. She had a job to do . . . and she had her Eric.

It is not always the case where a good secret intelligence agent has to blend in with the crowd. In fact, Ruby's carefully covered assets were sometimes an advantage . . . as they gave her an eager audience in the sterile domain of corporate business and within the drudgery of working with the diplomatic corps elite. Of course, there were some men who were not interested at all - an historical and surprisingly over-representation in the dangerous spy industry. She could not fathom why it was so.

The hardest part for her was to extricate herself from the tentacles of those who assumed privilege and were persistent nuisances, without causing too much offence. The foolhardy who did not care to recognise her subtle hints that she was spoken for, even during her role-playing classes, would suffer the inevitable painful kick to the left shin. This swift response combined with a frosty look of readiness indicated that a follow up with more convincing collateral damage was imminent. Such was her signature of disapproval.

"It's only training Ruby!" the assessor would bark out from the sidelines as the other students grinned.

"That's just what I'm doing," she would reply in a huff.

Her ability to speak Russian and Chinese was a bonus on the application proposal - as well as the recent active experience in helping MI6 to prosecute the Cigar Club. These darlings of the Whitehall brigade had finally been taken down for treason, mainly through Ruby's involvement in the baited outing of their activities led by Roger Davis . . . when she was only sixteen.

Ruby wanted to make amends now that Davis was gone and sometimes caught glimpses of his image staring back at her from amongst the crowd of people hurrying to their work places. It caused her pulse to race and her breathing to slow down enough to make her feel faint - but she did not.

She was determined to beat her acute and unexpected anxiety affliction on her own terms. Any record of having professional psychological help would indeed have destroyed her present public perception of her as the young hero.

Ruby questioned why it was, that so many young women would now testify without thinking, that she was as vulnerable as they perceived themselves to be. They had yet to learn about her strong determination and focussed mind-set to challenge such ingrained half-truths through action and example. Ruby's life was what she made it but it was Davis, who had provided the catalyst for her latest change.

Ruby had tried to find out as much as she could about him, now knowing that he had no immediate family or close friends except for work colleagues. Even though many of his counterparts in foreign lands had previously tried to kill him with vigour, they professionally respected and admired him.

After catching a taxi to the hotel, Ruby entered the familiar lounge bar and located the other four members of her party. She noticed that there was a new barman but nothing else had changed since her last visit to see Davis, so long ago. The staff at the hotel spoke highly of this quiet man with an analytical nature, except when he would spontaneously erupt into a funny character for an undercover assignment after having a few too many drinks.

The bar had been his safe haven, yet his dark secrets remained buried deep within. Of course, the people there did not know what he really did or would even have dared to ask, being across the river . . . across from Vauxhall Cross. Maybe Davis came across as the stereotypical sad comedian, living two opposing parallel lives and owning up to neither of them. Ruby's thoughts were interrupted, startling her.

"Excuse me Miss, but is your name Ruby Peters?" asked the barman quietly on hearing someone call out to her.

It was her shout again. With the small pay she was getting, buying five top-shelf drinks was beginning to bite into her role as the 'newbie", although most of the team knew about the reward of four diamonds given to her by that senior Chinese embassy official for her heroic capture of the 'Cigar Club'. The actual value of the diamonds was still unknown but their size and quality was often highly exaggerated to the extreme, which allowed Ruby to evade giving any answer at all.

Ruby looked towards the barman, thinking that it may be another official test of her reaction to being 'found out' in a public place. It had happened before in a live surveillance test.

The smile from the barman's weathered face, which advertised a rich life of service in the art of dispensing drinks and friendly banter with his regulars, soon had Ruby feeling more relaxed. She smiled back at him before examining her surroundings for anything or anyone unusual.

"Yes, it is. I am Ruby Peters. How can I help you?"

The barman walked away briskly around to the old-style cash register still used by the older clientele with real money and those not willing to leave a digital audit trail of their movements. He lifted up the cash drawer inside and produced a small white envelope. Ruby looked behind her to see if any of her work colleagues were watching. They were all too busy sculling their drinks ready for the next, making such a noise as to make those around them wonder, if maybe they had won the lottery.

The barman pushed the envelope across the bar covered by one hand, along with the tray of drinks. He looked straight ahead towards Ruby's friends as he leaned over and whispered closely above the noise.

"Here love. This was given to me by a close friend. We worked together over many years. He saved my life too . . . the only person I could trust. Now there's a fair piece of advice if you were to rely on those mates of yours."

Ruby paid for her drinks with a swipe card, stashing the envelope and her credit card into her bag as the barman resumed his duties with the group at the other end of the bar. He never looked back. She took the tray of drinks to her table much to the cheers from the three men and the ever-alert Mary.

"Do you know that barman Ruby . . . only he seemed to be having a few quiet words with you?"

"No, he was really quite nice about it actually . . . my credit card signature has worn down and he was telling me to get it fixed otherwise someone could write over the top of it," replied Ruby without hesitation, but with a smile that showed disapproval of her asking.

Mary was now a nuisance to be avoided. She was watching Ruby's every move like a hawk. The barman was right. By 10-30 pm, the function was becoming rather laboured, with the focus of attention on the life of Roger Davis beginning to wane.

They had heard or most likely guessed the fractured story of how Davis was killed in action, just outside the quaint English village of Dogbol where Ruby had lived. They knew she was partly to blame and looked quietly embarrassed as they scanned her up and down like a common criminal, through an occasional sideways glance.

They were told how Davis did not have time to fight back or to suffer much from the intruder's two bullets into his back. No one wants to die at the hands of a cowardly assassin . . . especially one from your own country.

Ruby's boyfriend Eric, the son of the Mayfair Mews Hotel owners, Robbie and Milly Johnson was not mentioned at all in the discussions even though he had rescued Ruby twice from the jaws of death. In fact, Ruby was carefully sidelined from any reference to her previous involvement with MI6 . . . loose lips and all that.

The Mayfair Mews located in Dogbol just up the road from Ruby's house and five miles from the larger town of Doulton was another starting point to make Ruby's mind wander into the past. Before she had met Davis, Eric was just another boy from school, although there was a hint that she may have liked him a little. She liked him much more after kissing him in front of 'Blizzard Face' and her friends and then seeing their reactions of jealousy and insecurity with their own standing.

Ruby thought back to the first time Davis had approached her. He had looked remarkably friendly for a government agent, although a bit ruffled and in disguise as a tradesman. He also seemed quite nervous – but then she was not quite seventeen and she was wearing her school uniform.

He had startled her at first by standing too close to her side at the bus stop before starting up a conversation by telling her all about her life and that he knew her father Harry was an ex-legionnaire. He talked quietly without really looking at her.

He proposed that it was probably the way her father viewed life which had prompted him to teach his daughter how to stand up to bullying, how to fight and even how to use a gun in the hope that she would never have to face the type of people that earlier times had dealt him.

Davis explained that matters of national importance required him to obtain information about two guests in the hotel and that she would be the best one to casually observe and report back to him without attracting any attention.

He explained that Eric was a bit too 'adventurous' and would definitely not win at poker with his expressive face. However, Ruby soon learnt that Eric too had been cajoled into the same assignment and had been given the codename of 'Diamond'.

To make matters worse, Eric had laughed at the choice of 'Scarlett' as her codename, if it had been deemed that she could even have one. Eric had tempted fate by continuing to giggle, thus sustaining a swift kick to his right leg . . . then the left one. Love, it is said can take many forms. Ruby had form.

All Davis required was the time when a guest came and went, registration numbers of vehicles and descriptions of visitors . . . but only when she was near the hotel, on normal visits. The school bus did stop right outside the hotel after all. Ruby's thoughts stopped in their tracks for a moment.

"It's time to finish up here in about ten minutes. We do have homes to go to and reputations to uphold," laughed Ben Williams, the analysis guru of their field team.

The Morpeth Arms was becoming too warm and fuzzy for Ruby as she was starting to drift her mind over what had gone wrong since the day she had accepted Davis's proposal to be his spy at the hotel. She wished that she could have that time over again . . . time to say a firm 'No!' to Davis and maybe kick him in the shin for approaching her like that. It may have saved his life. It would have saved her mind from the resulting total exhaustion, anxiety and recurrent nightmares about that one dark month of her life.

She hid her anxious thoughts well to avoid being hounded by doctors and shrinks with their prescription drugs, which she insisted, often made matters worse by causing addiction or thoughts of suicide. One of her close friends had been let down by such a lack of care, in favour of medication. She was only fourteen. Ruby never forgot Helen and assumed that her own aversion to professional help probably stemmed from the day Helen took her own life. She had wanted to get well.

Ruby thought about Eric. Would she have fallen in love with him if her life had just been so 'normal' and Eric had remained sheltered from all this spying business that had been thrust upon him? However, she had never been 'normal'. That was something for which she was eternally thankful.

"Are you ok there love?" whispered Mary calmly over the noise from the bar.

Mary was the only survivor of the shoot-out, which happened down the road from the Mayfair Mews. Davis was there with Barrie Barnes, a.k.a. 'Owl', to protect Ruby and her family who were thankfully not at home at the time.

The lead up to the surveillance was quite a complex scenario. Ruby had been kidnapped by Arab terrorists in order to blackmail Davis into allowing them to gain secret information about a nearby defence establishment. They had linked her to Davis merely by her being seen in his car with Eric.

The kidnapping had been ended by Eric and a Chinese spy named Tian 'The Taipan' who was one of the guests he was supposed to report on at the Mayfair Mews. Tian had shot and killed two of Ruby's abductors on a boat in Liverpool whilst helping Eric, but suffered a gunshot wound to her shoulder. At the same time, remote CIA operatives were marking that same boat with a drone, waiting for Scarab, the leader of the terrorist abductors to turn up. It was a completely different matter.

When the drone had analysed the scene, picking up images showing that two terrorists had been killed and that Scarab was walking down to below deck on the boat, the CIA decided to blow up the boat with the explosive-packed drone. The fathers of Eric and Ruby witnessed the violent explosion with the now befriended second person of interest at the Mayfair Mews, a certain Ilya Kasparov. They all thought that Eric and Ruby had died in the explosion.

Kasparov had rescued Tian after the boat explosion and had since formed a close relationship.

Unknown to anyone else, Eric and Ruby had run down to the end of the jetty and had jumped into the end boat to take cover from the initial shoot out before the explosion. Unlucky for them, this boat was also part of CIA operations run by rogue operatives who had stolen tens of millions of dollars in diamonds from the Arabs to trade for financing equipment for other private missions.

The boat headed off to Amsterdam unaware that they had stowaways, until Eric eased himself out of the forward anchor-hold. With Ruby's help, they managed to take over the boat whilst the agents were painting new registration numbers on the side of the boat from a dinghy. They then turned the boat around to head back to England, which is when all hell broke loose.

They were first attacked by members of the 'Cigar Club', an upper-crust gang of secret information sellers, in another fishing boat. Then the CIA turned up in a second boat. Finally, Tian and some Chinese Ninjas arrived in a third boat, backed up with a military helicopter. They all wanted those diamonds worth millions of dollars.

Through all the shooting, bombing and threatening behaviour, Ruby steered the boat violently and erratically, to ward off their attackers before the engine seized up and they had to abandon the boat. They continued their race for the coast in a dinghy.

At the last moment before being overwhelmed, the British Navy had arrived in full force to rescue them but not before Ruby had helped herself to some of the diamonds- the remainder confiscated by the British Government as 'treasure'. The boat and diamonds were now in their territory.

Ruby thought that her thirty-two diamonds would be compensation for her troubles. After all, the CIA had stolen them in the first place.

It was because of Ruby stealing some of the diamonds that Davis was monitoring Ruby's house for fear of reprisal on that fateful day, even though Ruby had just returned them. Davis later gave these diamonds to the Chinese embassy as compensation for them buying false information from the 'Cigar Club' in a sting and for being future witnesses at their trial.

On the sad day of the final shoot-out, two CIA operatives died, one of four youths sent to rob her house received a bullet in the leg, a Cigar Club member was killed and both Davis and his off-sider Barrie were both shot in the back at close range. They both died.

Eric's father, Robbie was also shot and badly wounded in his shoulder, which was the turning point in Ruby's desire to seek revenge on the elitist Cigar Club. The Chinese embassy then gave Ruby four diamonds back in return for her courage under fire during the demise of these crooks.

Ruby's vivid memory became a blur. Mary was shouting out to her, across the noisy bar.

"Ruby! Are you ok to go? We are all leaving."

It was getting near to closing time. Ruby's mind was spinning with regret and loss. Even having a few drinks did little to erase or dim any memories of her involvement in the death of Davis and so many others. She was now a different person from that gangly schoolgirl with the fringe and glasses who only had to deal with 'Blizzard Face' and her gang of social misfits at school.

Ruby took another quick glance at Mary who was still staring at her, relieved that she was about to take leave of Davis's colleagues who had been drinking heavily, spilling out their personal troubles to the rest of the group. She hated how they would occasionally glare at her and mumble cruel snippets to the others.

Ruby had already left the forget-me-not flowers for Davis at his grave that morning. They were the only bright but lonely sentinels marking the resting place of a hero, innocently beckoning a second look from every passer-by. Ruby was stuck in the past. The Morpeth Arms had that effect on her.

Mary could see that Ruby was in need of something more to calm her wretched state of mind . . . and to make her sleepy. They both walked up to the bar and sat down. The barman did not react to Ruby but made a mental note of the proceedings.

Another whiskey and coke was placed in front of her. Mary waved to the bar tender to swipe her credit card, knocking over her own drink, spilling whiskey onto Ruby's favourite dress. It looked intentional to the barman. He turned away without saying a word.

> "Sorry, love. I'll make sure you're into a taxi after this one. We all need to call it a day and move on with our lives. We will never forget our Roger . . . and you will always be a part of our team Ruby," offered Mary with a quick smile that turned into a suspicious stare.

A young man with jeans, tee shirt and black leather jacket had parked himself next to Ruby and was leaning very close towards her as he reached over her drink to retrieve his credit card from the barman who had returned to take a closer look at Mary. Ruby turned around quickly to catch his casual friendly gaze.

He smiled briefly. Yet in that split instant of awareness and calculation, there was something that seemed both familiar and yet so out of place. The young man got up to leave immediately without looking back. His drink remained at the bar, untouched.

Ruby looked towards Mary, who had followed him swiftly as he left the bar. He waved down a passing car from across the road, turning his face away as it passed by her. It was not a taxi. When Mary returned to the bar, she seemed to be a little tense.

> "Come on love, scull it down and I'll see you to your cab. There's a rank outside."

They both went outside to find a taxi dropping off a young woman. After confirming that it was free to hire, Ruby got in the front and gave the driver her address. Mary whispered Mary into her collar microphone.

> "She's away in a taxi. We may need to reconsider her suitability for this work. She's a right mess alright. Seen too much, too early and has a massive guilt complex over Davis."

There was a delay while her team leader worked out a solution. He pondered on the plan he was following.

"I'm surprised Mary. Well, I never expected such an outcome after looking through her test reports and training success. I'll set the wheels in motion to get her the help she needs. Monitor her from a distance and keep her away from any of our people for now. We need to create some space for her to think about her future. The usual Mary, you know, not much to do and lots of idle time. She won't take too kindly to being idle. Not that one."

"Aye OK then . . . oh, and there were a few incidents at the bar as well. Probably nothing, but one young guy got a bit too close to her, then abruptly left without touching his drink," replied Mary.

"He's not from Glasgow then eh, Mary."

The witty response allowed Mary to lighten-up. She shook her head, wondering if she had over-reacted, or was she maliciously creating a better case for seeing the end to Ruby's career?

Arriving outside her unit, Ruby was beginning to feel quite ill. After paying the relieved driver, she stumbled hurriedly out of the taxi, opened the front door with an electronic key transmitter, secured the unit by pressing the panic button on the wall and struggled frantically to reach the settee. It was 11-45pm.

She managed to find her mobile phone but it fell out of her trembling hands as she tried to cushion an impending free fall into doom. The next thing she remembered was rapidly drifting off to sleep, falling into a dark hole, just like the effects of the general anaesthetic that she had in hospital when her appendix had burst as a child. She collapsed onto the floor next to the settee, face-down, resting on her left arm. Her key chain was nearby.

The mobile phone rang out a familiar tune . . . the caller left the first of eight messages spaced throughout the night but Ruby remained motionless and silent . . . the recurrent dreams and worries no longer torturing her mind.

The living room lights turned off automatically, leaving the frozen outline of a young woman on the ground intermittently visible. The small green LED from her phone remained flashing all night long, like a sentinel calling out to a lost ship drifting away to the very limits of space.

At 2am and only ten miles away from Ruby's protected apartment, a lone figure wearing a three-quarter length winter coat was shielding his eyes, staggering along the middle of the road, breathing heavily and trying to remain upright. He was shouting out for someone to help him.

"Pozhaluysta, ne moye vremya umeret'!"

("Please, not my time to die!")

On any typical Friday night, it was not uncommon to have someone shout out abuse after being ejected from a taxi, with the driver eager enough to ditch his non-paying passenger onto any street. Many residents were asleep. Some didn't care anymore about a common nuisance. It was only on a Friday or Saturday night after all. But this night was different as was the ejected man who now found himself alone and incapacitated.

Out of the darkness, bright lights pierced his heavy eyes. They were getting brighter and the noise of something coming towards him made him stop . . . and slowly drop to his knees. The feeling of an almost expected outcome writhed within his fractured thoughts, now swirling over the events in his life: girlfriends, family . . . loneliness, people and faces . . . shattered bodies . . . and Tian, the love of his life. The dull heavy thud of the massive impact and the fracturing of glass prompted wary residents to at least peek outside from beyond their curtained windows.

A small silver car reversed slowly, back over the body in the road, the female driver checking to make sure that this man was never going to get up again. This driver was not in any hurry to leave, according to witnesses.

Finally, with a screech of its tyres and high revving of the engine, the car spun around in a tight curve and raced towards the bottom of the street and around the corner.

The street became still for a few moments, until reassured by the movements from emboldened neighbours, front lights turned on and doors slowly opened up onto the horrific scene. Hushed voices drowned out by the echo of police cars and a lone ambulance making their way towards the man in the three-quarter length winter coat were whispering comments about the still body . . . now unrecognisable and torn apart.

His blood, as indeed his solitary way of life, had drained to ebb away in a foreign land, on a cold, black bitumen road. He was all alone in death.

For the London Metropolitan Police it was just another typical Friday night. Ruby Street was in lockdown. The police cordoned off the area, marked key findings with tags for forensics while the ambulance slowly wandered up the street. There is never any rush to get to the morgue.

A black unmarked car pulled up in a rush. A security pass flashed by the face of the police, to give sole access to the body. The police had strict orders to keep all reporters and bystanders away.

However, one reporter already had his story. He was hurriedly transmitting it to his office, along with photos of the accident scene . . . and the body. After his gear smashed to the ground, he was roughly taken aside for questioning.

He had arrived a little too soon and MI6 wanted to know why . . . and for whom he was working.

# The Raid

S aturday morning on the motorway was as busy as usual for Eric who was rushing back to London in his BMW. He needed to find out why Ruby had not answered his phone messages.

The security device that he had installed in her unit had instantly contacted him as an SMS the moment she had pressed the panic button at 11-45pm. Eric had previously told her that by pressing the button, her unit would become her safe-house but she only thought that the device was just to secure the premises. Eric had also installed cameras linked to his cloud storage.

This was the second time that Eric had responded to one of Ruby's emergencies, the first being after her kidnapping in Dogbol. The homing beacon in her hairgrip had saved her life by identifying her exact location for Eric and Tian to rescue her. That ended with three terrorists dying, a massive boat explosion and the fiasco on the high seas, chased by three different and determined groups of attackers.

As Eric approached his unit, two police cars and a black sedan with flashing lights overtook him. He slowed down his approach to find the cars had stopped right outside the unit, with heavily armed police racing to secure the building perimeter. His rear view mirror showed an ambulance parked at the top of the road, which was not a good sign. He decided to wait a while longer and phoned Ruby again. There was a delay. She finally picked up but sounded hesitant.

"Eric? Is that you Eric?"

"Ruby, what's going on? The police are outside your unit. You didn't return any of my calls. You activated the panic button. Are you OK? What's happening?"

Ruby made some faint noises and Eric could hear the banging on her door in the background.

"Police! Police! Open up the door and be quick about it. Open the door now. This is the police. We are armed."

Eric decided to stay in the car. He knew that Ruby was Ok, although she sounded a little groggy.

"I . . . I have to go . . . to get the door Eric . . . Keep away," offered Ruby as she headed wearily to the door.

She instinctively reached for the hair-grip attached with putty to the side of a picture frame. She placed it carefully, deep into her ruffled hair. Eric had given it to her as a present after their first dinner date. It was a homing device linked to his phone.

Looking through the peephole, she could see a group of police officers waiting at the door. Releasing the door lock was met with an overwhelming response, with the door being forced open violently by the Tactical Response Team. Plain-clothes officers with two others wearing white forensic suits and a police dog also burst into the unit.

Ruby was quickly secured with handcuffs and read her rights. She now fully comprehended that her arrest was for something very serious. There was no mention of any charge as a police officer asked her some immediate questions.

> "Are you Ruby Peters and is your vehicle a silver colour VW Golf, registration number DGH-45-H?"

Ruby was still waking up and feeling quite drowsy.

> "Yes. I am Ruby Peters and yes that is my car . . . it's always parked at the front of the building," replied Ruby, waving her hand towards the front window.

A uniformed police officer with three pips on his arm looked at her sternly.

> "And is this your electronic car opener?" he asked sharply.

Ruby could not focus on what he had said. A senior plainclothes officer looked at her dishevelled clothes and smudged makeup. She still had the aroma of a late night bar. He didn't need to make any obvious comments. It was the way he looked at her, that spoke a thousand words.

> "You will have to come down to the station to be interviewed Miss Peters so that we can verify your activities over the last twenty four hours . . . and to take a drug and alcohol test."

> "But what have I done? I went out last night, came home by taxi and fell asleep on the settee. I . . . I may have had my drink spiked," replied Ruby lazily.

The police dog was scratching around the settee as they led her away. Meanwhile, a team of forensic experts ransacked Ruby's unit in a most methodical way.

> "Wait, you can't do that. Where's your warrant? I have done nothing wrong. I want you to call my superiors. Look at my ID and see who I work for," argued Ruby.

They took no notice as one of the officers grabbed the back of her neck and a handful of her hair, navigating her quickly outside onto the pavement before bundling her roughly into the back seat of the black sedan, which then drove off at high speed.

Eric had parked just up the street from the unit, watching the area buzzing with police cars and inquisitive bystanders. He could see two photographers snapping wildly to get anything that moved in front of them. They had arrived on a motorbike, presumably before the police had turned up, which would normally have seemed rather odd to the trained eye.

Eric thought nothing of it at the time as his mind was racing. He had to be very careful not to interfere with any police, defence or intelligence agency operations, as that would be the end of his career requiring top-level security clearance. He also had to ensure that his sometimes-wayward antics did not in any way affect Ruby's own 'intelligence service security clearance' or compromise her position, by forming any association with undesirable people, foreign powers or illegal businesses. Finally, he had learnt his lesson.

Things were more complicated this time around, because just as Ruby was now working for MI6, Eric was part of a defence electronics project at a secret location in the countryside. Today was a Saturday and he had the weekend off.

He usually visited Ruby at what was their home base every weekend, after staying at the project site during the week. Sometimes however, he would be away travelling or testing prototype equipment at military locations in the UK or overseas.

He now looked stunned to have seen a shabby, drowsy-looking Ruby arrested by the police and bundled quite forcibly into the unmarked car. She was in handcuffs too. That alone raised his suspicions about the seriousness of the situation. His monitoring device was registering that Ruby had activated her hairgrip transmitter, so he was now able to discreetly track her movements.

"She must be really worried about her safety," he murmured, trying to think of what else to do besides following the black car without being seen.

He texted Ruby's father during the trip, whilst stopping at the various traffic lights. It was in a specially encrypted code that he had devised only for their small family group and a few trusted 'outsiders'. Her father, Harry Peters just happened to be in London, working around the docks on behalf of a client from France. He alternated between Glasgow, London and Liverpool using his expertise in importing and exporting to solve client's logistics problems. This also included customs and warehousing of valuable cargoes.

Harry had supplied many of their close friends with permanent jobs that occasionally involved dangerous encounters with some quite nasty people. Harry also worked with Port Customs. It was very handy that Harry and Eric's father, Robbie Johnson had earlier military backgrounds with the French Foreign Legion. Their transition from mercenary soldiers to business partners must have been acceptable to MI6, otherwise Eric and Ruby would not have obtained their clearances to work for defence and intelligence components within the government.

Eric also knew Tian, or 'Taipan", the Chinese foreign agent whose father was at the high end of the Chinese Embassy in London. Tian and Ilya Kasparov the Russian General who was probably a foreign agent had both helped to put the 'Cigar Club' away by giving evidence against them at a special closed-door trial. Eric considered them as 'non-threatening'. Eric and Ruby had also witnessed Tian and Ilya develop a somewhat close relationship whilst keeping their unusual business practices separate. Love it seems has no bounds.

Now was not the time for Eric to complicate the situation by contacting either of them with a view to helping Ruby – if in fact there was any problem. Maybe it was some sort of training. All he could establish was that Ruby had been taken in for questioning but had not returned his phone calls after activating the panic button in their unit . . . and yet she had activated her personal tracking device. Eric had assumed that it was the police or her own MI6 people who were at the unit, but assuming anything was not likely to bring him closer to the truth. He preferred to see at firsthand what was going on.

"Mary! I'll give Mary Turner a private call to see if she knows anything about it," Eric whispered to himself.

Mary had supported Eric at the hospital after his father had been shot on that day Davis was killed, but her often-public showing of distaste for Ruby was probably due to her partly blaming Ruby for Davis's death. Ruby thought that Mary probably had a 'thing' for Roger but had suppressed her desire to make it known to him.

"Yes, hello, how can I help you?" answered Mary politely.

She hadn't recognised his project phone number and why would she? They had not spoken for at least eighteen months.

"Mary, Eric Johnson here. Mary, I need your help in determining if Ruby is in trouble. She has just been arrested and taken away in an unmarked car . . . and there are three police cars at my unit as well," gushed Eric.

Mary seemed stuck for an answer . . . or did not want to say.

"Look Eric, I don't know how much you know about Ruby's last twenty four hours, but it appears that she may have had too much to drink last night and . . . and well it looks as though she may have done some very bad things . . . I can't tell you anymore. Look, just relax and go home. I'll let you know when I find out some more details . . . so go home for now. I am sure it will amount to nothing . . . but then she did seem a bit delusional last night. I put her in a cab myself. She may be having a nervous breakdown."

Mary terminated the call leaving Eric's mind racing for answers. He now knew that MI6 and the police were those involved with her arrest, but the facts just did not add up.

"No way is she having a breakdown. Not my Ruby."

He kept following Ruby's signal from the black car as it veered away from the city, heading off towards Cheltenham. It dawned on Eric that they were headed towards GCHQ, the coding and communications division of British Intelligence.

He would have to make sure that Ruby's signals and the location of his receiver did not give his identity or position away. Eric had a cunning plan for that eventuality. He loved to anticipate future events, never forgetting what Roger Davis had told him about Ruby's kidnapping.

"There's no such thing as coincidence. What we have is contrivance and a well-made plan . . . and therefore an audit trail for us to unlock the past and discover their weaknesses."

As Eric was driving cautiously about one mile distance from the black car, Harry Peters sent a coded signal back to Eric's phone as a series of letters, numbers and symbols. Eric reached into his pocket for his private phone and dialled up Harry directly. Each phone had a matched reciprocal scrambler so they could talk freely, but still guardedly.

"Ruby's people have arrested her for questioning and have her in an unmarked car that I am following. Looks like Cheltenham. She activated her unit panic button last night but did not pick up the phone or respond to my messages. Before her arrest, she activated her personal tracking device. I called Mary from MI6 but she is probably hoping that Ruby is having a nervous breakdown," said Eric.

There was a delay of about two minutes.

"Taken care of muster. See you near destination. Possible three more elves and your own pop. Stay calm. Gain more data for us to act. Looks like we're back into the saddle laddie."

Harry had the situation under control and Eric was relieved that he had things moving. The next step was to find where in Cheltenham she had been detained . . . and why. Sure enough, the transmitter from Ruby's hairgrip indicated that the black car had reached that familiar doughnut-shaped GCHQ complex.

Eric quickly pulled over near one of the shops, about one mile from GCHQ, placing a second receiver on the rear of a waiting bus, which was just about to move off. He then went back to his car to turn off the primary receiver after checking that it still showed Ruby to be in the GCHQ building, in a particular section. The signal stopped just before he turned it off . . . they were on to him alright.

"I hope they follow that bus all the way back to London," he whispered with a grin.

Eric walked across the road to get a coffee, sat down near the window and texted a new code to Harry. The reply came back that he had thirty minutes more to wait before he could join up with his old team. Then another text came through. He looked at it with disbelief.

"No . . . no, Ruby wouldn't do that! This has to be a setup. She wouldn't kill our friend Ilya Kasparov. No . . . it can't be," he stuttered quietly.

With tears in his eyes thinking of Ilya, and how Tian would react, Eric ran back across the road to his car and replied to the message by texting his privately scrambled phone number. The phone rang immediately. He grabbed it nervously, steeling himself for that familiar voice to shout and scream at him . . . but there was silence.

"Tian? . . . Tian, are you there?" he asked cautiously.

"Why, Eric? Why did she do this to my Ilya? Just tell me what you know before I can even think what I am to do about this. We had become like sisters. My father thinks of her as his daughter. Where is she Eric?" she replied quietly.

"Oh Tian, you must know she didn't do it. I can't believe that Ilya has been killed. There is no way. She has been set up. I know it because she activated the unit panic button last night then didn't return my calls . . . and . . . and then this morning she used the tracking device to warn me that she was being taken away and feared for her safety. We both know that she could not do such a thing. Please Tian."

"Where? Where have they taken her Eric and who has taken her? Let's start from there!" she demanded with more force.

"MI6 have taken her to GCHQ in Cheltenham and police forensics are ransacking our unit as we speak. I don't know any more. I have only just arrived from my work in the country and all this has just happened. I do know that she was going to the pub to remember Roger Davis at a reunion last night . . . the pub across the river. It was just her work colleagues.

But wait on . . . if she activated the panic button last night, then there will be video footage of the living room . . . three frames per second until it uses all the memory . . . why that's a good thirty hours' worth streamed to my personal account on the cloud. I can access it from anywhere but trust me Tian . . . she has not done this to Ilya. Why would she? She liked him and he was the one who helped us both as you know."

Tian's thoughts moved from imagining the horrendous scene of Ilya's killing, to remembering her close dealings with Ruby and Eric and their families. She was hurting badly.

"Yes, of course I always believe you Eric. I had to ask you to verify what I had heard from the Russian communications channel. People will pay dearly for this grave mistake. The time for grieving is not now . . . now is the time to seek out and punish those responsible. Check your video and let me know what you find."

"But how . . . how did it happen, Tian?"

"They ran him down with a car like an animal. The Russians tell me that someone drugged him to make him drowsy. They say that it was a woman driving the car . . . and that she appeared drunk. The time on a surrounding video shows 2am, but too much coincidence and what are the odds of her driving into Ilya, without it being contrived by her or by others? And yet, they say they have photo evidence of a woman's face in the windscreen of her car. It was her car Eric. So tell me . . . is the car damaged Eric?"

"I . . . I never checked because I didn't know about the accident Tian. I will download the video from my unit and get back to you. There is also a camera, which monitors her car on the road . . . just as long as she parked it in the same spot. I am so sorry Tian. My dad was a great friend of Ilya. He will be very upset at all this going on. I am so very sorry."

Eric was feeling sick inside. How could Ruby have snapped and gone out of her way to run down Ilya after drugging him, immediately after being with MI6 people at the pub . . . and after she said that she was going to catch a taxi there and back?

It didn't make sense. Eric began to think of who would have been at the pub with Ruby. Mary was there for sure . . . but who else could verify how she was acting and how she got home. Did she take her car? He had forgotten to check its position on the street outside the unit.

Eric started to download the unit security video to his portable computer. As it was downloading, he sampled some of the packets of video data. The first video clip started at exactly11-34 pm - the time when she pressed the panic button. The split screen shows the living room and yes, Ruby had parked the car in its usual spot. Eric stared at the screen hoping for a miracle.

The first few seconds showed Ruby stumbling towards the settee, briefly trying to stand up straight, before falling onto her knees and then collapsing face-down into the rug in front of the settee. Her key chain was near to her still body.

> "Wow, she's out like a light. That is not the result of drinking . . . unless she is ill . . . but wait . . . yes, the car is outside and the unit securely locked. No one can get in and she obviously will not be going out in a hurry," muttered Eric as he was trying to zoom in on Ruby and then the car.

Suddenly he stopped muttering and zoomed back onto the car. The back window was half-open! He knew this because he could see the cushion in the middle of the back seat. With tinted windows, it is impossible to see into the car at night and he could see that cushion so clearly.

Next, he zoomed in to where Ruby had collapsed. He highlighted the key chain and then zoomed in further to examine it. The unit front door opener was there.

Eric had given her a radio control door opener so that the locks would open automatically, in order that she could just run into the unit and press the panic button if anything went wrong.

She had done just that! Eric made out several keys but looking closely . . . the electronic car fob was different. He would recognise hers immediately because she had a red spot painted on both sides, for 'Scarlett' at his request to distinguish it from his own, which had a white spot for 'Diamond'. Someone had done a switch on her and used her car.

The next thing was to pick the video clip which would be somewhere near 2am, around the time Ilya was killed and then one which would be say 8am – just before the police arrived. He examined these clips and found that Ruby had not moved since she collapsed at least until after 2am – and she was still semi-collapsed on the settee at 8am.

Checking the clips for the car – it was missing at 2am but back in a different position at 8am. Someone had taken it between when she had collapsed, and 2am . . . and then it was returned but out of place.

Eric realised that he had not only proved that Ruby was not to blame but that he also had video evidence of who took the car. He started going through the footage, watching for when the car was not there. At 12-48am he stopped the frame and zoomed in on the person who was standing near the car.

A few frames further on and it was clear that this person was the same person who stole the car. He highlighted the best shot of the person's face as it caught the street lighting. He let out a scream.

> "Oh my god, Oh my god . . . it's Mary Turner! You bitch! You framed my Ruby and probably killed Ilya. She never liked you much . . . and obviously with good reason."

He went through the remainder of the frames quickly to establish when the car had returned. There it was . . . 4-22am, parked a good ten feet out of position – something that Ruby would never do without texting him. It was just another thing that Eric had insisted on, to give him an external visual message that things were alright in the unit, if he drove past.

Eric now had some startling information for Harry Peters who was bringing Eric's father and three more 'friends' to meet him in Cheltenham. He couldn't imagine what they would do at this early stage to clear Ruby without giving away the visual evidence, for there may be more people like Mary at MI6 who were involved.

Eric also sent Tian a coded message that he had proof that Ruby was innocent, that he knew who stole her car . . . and that she should meet up with him and his team at Cheltenham. He then checked the images of the car at 8am and zoomed in the front left-hand side. Yes, it had some major damage to the bonnet. The headlight assembly was broken too.

He was staring at the murder weapon ... and it belonged to his girlfriend.

# Michael

It was now 1pm on that same overcast Saturday. The time agreed upon by Ruby's rescue team, organised by Eric, to meet up and plan for a rescue. It seemed that events like this were becoming far too frequent, involving the same players with only the time and place changing. This time they had experience on their side. Eric's clear video evidence would prove that Ruby had been framed.

As many people know, dealing with the likes of any insular government department can be most frustrating, but having evidence to show that one of their own intelligence officers was complicit in framing another one of their kind calls for a little time out. Time to assess the reality of getting a fair and transparent result while they flounder in damage control

However, this was not a simple case of shoplifting, but the murder of a senior foreign agent on British soil, one who had diplomatic immunity and whose embassy would now be directly in touch with the prime minister.

In addition, someone had leaked the story to the local media, naming names and insinuating that MI6 had eliminated a high-ranking double agent from its organisation. The situation was developing into a major international embarrassment for the Russians, with still unknown consequences for the British Government and for Ruby.

Meanwhile, Ruby had recovered from her drowsy and somewhat incoherent state of mind. After freshening up, they gave her a cooked breakfast before presenting her before a senior lone official in an overly warm interview room. He looked familiar. Yes, she recognised him as the same suited man who had interviewed her at the debriefing session – the same day that the Navy had rescued them, three years before.

He was a sinister figure because of his bland looks and almost catatonic poses. He also had a calculating method of talking quietly with many lengthy pauses, designed to make her edgy and prone to make her blurt out anything, in order to end the torment to her mind.

"Hello Ruby. Well, we meet once more under a cloud of suspicion and . . . anticipation . . . on both sides."

Ruby looked at him briefly, then at the two-way mirror on the wall to their left side. She sighed and shook her head at what was likely to be a lengthier interview than last time. Looking back at his frozen staring face, she noticed that he had that fixed stare which never seemed to blink or flinch.

"Do you know why you are here?" he asked solemnly.

Ruby remained silent. She was weighing up where this interview was headed. As a potential agent of MI6, for her to be bundled into a car and taken for questioning without them charging her or telling her anything about her predicament was way beyond normality, even for MI6 protocol . . . unless it was more of their spontaneous training. She would have preferred a late stay in bed until noon. It was Saturday after all . . . her time.

Ruby smiled at him then lowered her head before rising slowly to her feet. She closed her eyes and stretched her frame like a cat as if preparing to deliver one of her flying head-kicks. This move always seemed to unsettle anyone who was trying to get the better of her. The man was not looking at her, or was the least bit interested in her silly antics.

'One can never underestimate the strengths of an opponent who is prepared to strike back at their leisure,' was the essence of her martial arts training according to her teacher.

The man appeared unmoved, possibly having had the same teacher. His hand moved slowly towards the edge of the desk from where he retrieved the envelope, given to Ruby by the barman at the hotel. She glanced at it briefly before breathing out slowly, releasing all her tension.

"Please sit down until you are told to stand. This is not a game," he said quietly, waving his hand containing the envelope.

Ruby remembered being given the envelope but had been so overcome with tiredness due to an obvious case of drink spiking, that she had not retrieved it from her handbag. She sat down slowly, reaching out for the envelope. The man dropped it on the table, before quickly slapping his hand over it, causing Ruby to instinctively recoil.

"Can you explain how you came by this letter?"

Ruby had endured enough of this childish game of bluff.

"Why am I here and why have you not told me what charges . . . if any . . . I am being persecuted over? You have kidnapped me from my home, ransacked my unit and all without a warrant or my permission," she replied quickly but firmly, staring at the man and his continuing passive display of superiority.

He got up slowly and walked towards the door. As the door opened, he stopped, looking back at her analytically.

"You are suspected of murdering Ilya Kasparov by running him over with your car. You have a letter in your possession from Roger Davis, who it seems is reaching out from the grave to give you . . . you, Ruby Peters . . . a coded message regarding a highly confidential list of MI6 double-agents."

He paused, smiled briefly whilst walking back to her, placed the letter on the desk then left the room quickly, leaving her alone to her thoughts. Ruby thought that this had to be a training exercise. Yet, she was quite sure that they would not joke about such a serious matter. The very idea that her car had indeed killed her friend Ilya was too shocking in the extreme. It was also in bad taste.

However, was there a minute possibility that she may have had a psychotic episode or something else to explain her actions, she wondered. That is if she was responsible as they were alleging. After all, she did collapse and was comatose all night long.

A quick rethink of the previous night soon put things back into perspective. Sure, she had gone to the function and returned home by taxi. She had activated the panic switch, thus locking herself in the unit just before she collapsed . . . and she had only just recovered when Eric phoned her, immediately before the police arrived. How could she be in two places at once?

She did not know for sure if what this man had said was true but it was becoming more and more unlikely. It now did not feel like a training session, yet there was something very wrong with the whole situation when viewed from any analytical angle. At least Eric was aware of what was going on. She knew that he would have set the wheels in motion to get the help she needed, reaching out to the only people she and Eric could trust – her much suffering but devoted family.

It was too early to start grieving for Ilya, if he had in fact been murdered, which led to her deduction that Tian would now be somewhere in the shadows, poised to avenge his death if it was true. She would be devastated but ready to act immediately.

Ruby removed the letter from the envelope, which had remained sealed until MI6 had retrieved it from her handbag. She unravelled the single piece of paper they had obviously looked at and just as certainly, had not been able to understand, hence its return to Ruby. She touched the paper gently as if Davis had somehow left part of his spirit trapped within its fibres, asking herself why he would leave her such an important document.

Ruby narrowed her eyebrows on seeing that the message consisted of a drawing and some random words and numbers. She looked straight ahead before turning her gaze towards the two-way mirror. They really wanted Eric. As she turned to look at the piece of paper again, the man came back into the room and put his hand on her shoulder softly.

> "It's all true Ruby. Kasparov is dead . . . and your car was the weapon used in the hit and run. This is not part of any training to see how well you hold up in an uncomfortable interview with tragic consequences or made-up charges. This is very real," he said with what seemed genuine sadness.

Ruby was shocked that Ilya may have actually been murdered. Now they were blaming her, without her even having a credible alibi. She had been alone and was under the influence of drugs.

> "It wasn't me," replied Ruby quietly, "Ilya was a close friend of mine and helped to put away the 'Cigar Club'. He rescued me from them when I tried to . . . to kill them all, for taking Roger Davis away from us . . . all because of my silly diamonds."

The man looked at the tears forming in her eyes.

"That's all I wanted to hear Ruby. We already knew that it was not you. After all, we do not hire psychotic murderers you know . . . but we may create them, given enough time it would seem. The perpetrators are playing mind games with us.

They even chose Ruby Street for their display of revenge, which leads me to think that they will make a mistake sooner than later . . . being so personally affected by their grievances."

He appeared to be showing a complete change in personality as he touched her hand and nodded his head before walking back to his chair. He smiled at her again. It looked genuine.

"Kasparov's murder could have been an international disaster Ruby, so we took our action to show that we were on top of the situation based on the original evidence, provided so efficiently to the Russians. So . . . how is that smart boyfriend of yours then . . . Eric Johnson? Now there's someone we could do with in this section."

Ruby looked at him defensibly. Was he playing games again?

"Ah yes, Eric . . . he's already mobilised the troops and sent off our own clowns on a bus trip to London it would seem. We are waiting for him and his followers to contact us once they realise it is their only way of providing us with the evidence, proving that you are innocent of all charges . . . so that we can actually pursue who we are really after," he continued matter-of-factly.

"And the letter, what was all that about the letter?" snapped Ruby, interrupting his light banter.

"Call me Michael . . . you will be working closely with me from now on. You have now been re-assigned to me, my dear Miss Peters. Highly irregular of course . . . but right up your alley I would imagine . . . going against procedure and establishment. I think we had that sort of discussion last time . . . am I right?"

Ruby remained guarded in her approach. Was he trying to work out some 'good cop, good reward' methodology for finding out just what her price was for information and betrayal?

"The letter . . . Michael . . . why would Roger Davis give me a letter . . . or what looks like some fanciful game or riddle . . . that contains a clue to our country's double-agents. I mean, do you really think that I am some sort of village idiot or something? We are at GCHQ, the home of communications and cryptic codes and all those desk-bound data-crunching nerds. Why even Eric would be able to sort out your magic letter without any of your billion-dollar enterprise efforts," replied Ruby sarcastically.

Michael looked surprised.

"Exactly, just what we thought too. Now all we need is the man himself . . . the letter is authentic by the way . . . and what it stands for, unfortunately . . . or fortunately now that we have it. It's a pity that Roger had come to the sad conclusion that you were the only person he could trust and that Eric was the only one who could interpret the code . . . should anything happen to him."

"And it did . . . he's dead," replied Ruby bitterly.

Ruby was beginning to see reason in what Michael had told her. It was too fanciful to be made-up, especially by the likes of MI6, unless they had enlisted a team of overly enthusiastic scriptwriters.

"My terms Mister Whitehall, are that if you meet Eric, it needs to be in a public place, with only yourself and no backup support – and of course me. I need to go home with him or at least to a safe house whilst all this is sorted and I want safety protection for my poor family. I'm sure Eric will have made provision for securing his information, to be used with maximum damage should anyone . . . get out of line," demanded Ruby with a firm steady pace.

Before Michael could reply, Ruby had one more important message to express.

"So . . . how do you expect to protect your witnesses or this critical and sensitive information or sideline these suspected moles, using your own people, who may themselves be double-agents or informers? Answer me that . . . Michael."

"That's the nature of our deceptive broken world Ruby. But we do have some special people to take care of that . . . totally beyond reproach I assure you . . . hand-chosen by 'C' himself."

Ruby imagined that they would be the ones who could be the biggest threat to the organisation, controlling everything and eliminating all those who would try to expose them. She looked at his expression. Michael did not look too sure himself as he looked towards the two-way mirror, thinking quietly about Henry Roberts, his supervisor and his obsessive demand to retrieve that list for himself.

"And my special people, well I have my family Michael. So, let me call Eric and we will see how well he has hidden his location. He is never where you expect him to be of course and thankfully, I never doubt that he has found some way of finding me."

"A Diamond for a Ruby is what he is, albeit a rough diamond at that. He needs to be brought into the fold I think. We already know where he is Ruby. Of course we know. That's what we do," whispered Michael with a smile and a wink.

Ruby was thinking that she had been conned and he had spoken down to her. Sure, everything was all rosy now. Yet, only two hours ago, she was forcibly removed from her unit and accused of murder. Then there was the night before . . . the drink spiking. She wondered who had done this to her and why. Michael looked so smug. It seemed to her, that he thought he had tamed her resentment for him and the 'company'.

Suddenly, Michael got up and went over to the two-way mirror. He closed the curtains briskly on each side of the mirror after waving whoever was there to finish the interview session. She could not know that Henry Roberts' had been watching her or that he now had a worried expression as he marched out of that room in a temper, reaching for his phone.

Ruby steeled herself to strike Michael down if he thought that it was time for a stronger approach. She was not going to let him touch her. He came over to her slowly and sat on the side of the desk looking away from her, trying to look non-threatening.

"We don't keep any more secrets between us now that I want you to be working closely with me . . . but let me tell you a few things about your behaviour Ruby Peters, which is partly due to your age and inexperience. You work for us now. We want you to live long and prosper and have a balanced life . . . not to join Roger Davis in that gloomy cemetery patch that you visit each month."

Ruby was getting mad and kept trying to interject but he kept talking softly, monotonously.

"You made a grave mistake last night. Yes, it was such a simple mistake, but one that nearly cost you your life. You drank that last whisky and coke . . . even after you had looked that young man in the eyes. Even after he had reached over your drink . . . and then you didn't contact your supervisor to let him know that you had been drinking and were feeling unwell . . . and that you had been deposited into a taxi by Mary Turner, supposedly out of concern for your wellbeing."

Ruby was feeling as though her career had just ended.

"I . . . I don't know what to say to you. It was a terrible mistake and my being with you here is all the evidence I need to know that if I was on an assignment . . . then I would probably be dead right now."

Michael looked at Ruby closely and then rose to his feet.

"Perhaps you'd like to meet that man from last night Ruby . . . he is one of our own. He relied upon your inexperience to slip you a spike in your drink . . . and right in front of Mary too, but then she had more important things on her mind."

"You poisoned me? Then wrecked my apartment looking for what . . . the diamonds? And now, you probably have Eric and then god knows who else is looking for me, risking their lives for me again!" screamed Ruby.

Michael looked a little unsettled. He turned towards her with a more worried look. His breathing seemed shallow.

"You have been used to do MI6 business Ruby Peters. You have actually done more for your country by being asleep than all of us at GCHQ could do with our PR spin and frantic calls to calm down the President of the Russian Federation," he replied almost apologetically.

"And what are you going to tell me now . . . Michael . . . that I have secret powers when I'm asleep and turn into some sort of angel of death? What about Ilya? Why did he have to die? Was that your business too?"

Michael sat down again and banged the desk as he stared at her causing Ruby to fear he would strike her.

"Right, don't say another word until I've finished. Here is the full story of what went down last night . . . no holds barred and this will be the only time that you will have such occasion as to question what we do or how we do it. OK Ruby?" he shouted.

Ruby was surprised at his sudden anger and just nodded.

"We heard through our contacts yesterday afternoon, that you were going to be targeted at Roger's remembrance last night at the Morpeth Arms. Apparently, the party was arranged by persons now known to us, to be solely for the purpose of getting you drunk before taking advantage of that fact whilst you slept at home. They were to use your identity and your car to murder an important double agent of ours . . . yes Ruby, your friend Ilya Kasparov. He worked for us you know, recruited by your good friend Davis. We miss him too. He was a good friend of mine. If I thought you had done it, then you would not be sitting here in front of me."

Ruby stopped herself from speaking.

"If our man hadn't drugged you so that you remained under our surveillance, for us to pick you up in the morning with great fanfare, then you may have found yourself wiped out in some unfortunate accident . . . carried out in retribution for Ilya's death. We created an alibi for you, to give to the Russians who were notified immediately . . . but what we can't work out is why that barman was killed . . . any ideas about that Ruby?"

Ruby remembered the friendly barman passing her the envelope saying it was from a friend. She put it out of her mind to concentrate on the matter at hand, not knowing if she could trust Michael. She did not answer, but she also could not restrain herself anymore.

"Why was all this set up in the first place . . . and why Ilya?"

"Because it looks like someone wants to eliminate you and Eric and all those involved in the 'Cigar Club' fiasco, including the members themselves . . . but the question of double-agents raises its head again which leaves me to think they may be one and the same problem.

We need to put an end to this Ruby, or else you are going to be watching over your shoulders for the rest of your life . . . and because you are one of us, you have our full support to stop this right now. But you have to be straight with us and not play silly games with Eric . . . for all his good intentions. We have to get hold of that list and deal with the names on it. We can't function efficiently with double-agents handling our classified information."

Ruby looked away then turned back towards him with a look of horror.

"My Eric is in real trouble . . . you have to save him."

Michael walked towards the door, which had just released its locking mechanism.

"I'll send him in to you in a moment Ruby with the rest of your loyal friends . . . oh, but one of the 'fantastic four' escaped again as per usual. She is just like you

Ruby . . . young, beautiful and headstrong with a very stubborn streak . . . perhaps a little less unpredictable."

Ruby looked puzzled.

"I think you call her the 'snake lady'. She is not allied to anyone it would seem except to her father . . . a strange woman indeed but a deadly force to be reckoned with!"

Ruby smiled and wiped her eyes as it dawned on her who this person might be.

"Tian"

"Oh yes . . . now there's a problem in itself Ruby. Your name has been outed to the public, what with those damn reporters being party to the game. So maybe we are going to have to call you by another name. What's your middle name . . . or your grandmother's name on your mother's side . . . that eliminates your old surname," he pondered.

Ruby smiled broadly.

"You can call me Scarlett if you like . . . just that . . . Scarlett."

Michael let out a deep sigh as he walked down the corridor, thinking about what her fellow recruits would say about that. He strode past the guarded doorway of interview room 'Delta 4' before stopping to walk back. He peeked through the observation glass, thought for a moment, then gestured for the officer to open the door.

Eric and Ruby's father Harry were talking with their three friends who had jumped at the chance of seeing some real action again. These ex-legionnaires were once part of Harry's platoon along with Eric's father, Robbie Johnson. Harry turned around slowly, with his surprise met with an open-mouthed stare, by the ever-observant Eric.

"You old rascal Harry . . . still up to the job I see."

"Aye, you never forget how to look after your mates or a head-strong daughter Mike. I presume my Ruby is in with you and has been unharmed," replied Harry warily, getting up to shake his hand.

Michael looked at the others in the group and then stared at Eric as he answered back.

"Ruby is just fine by the way if not a little rattled by all this. Now that she works for us, she gets looked after by us . . . although that is something that flies against what she has been brought up to believe eh, Harry. So, you must be Eric then?"

Eric had taken the spare homing receiver out of his rucksack and was trying to work out why it was not working. He was too busy to acknowledge Michael. Harry was not surprised.

"We must be in a Faraday cage," whispered Eric excitedly to an uninterested Harry.

"I hope you're not going to attach that to anything in our car park. We still have an agent following your primary device to London on that bus. Oh . . . and I like the video clips of your unit and Ruby's car . . . very smart Eric. You have single-handedly cleared Ruby all by yourself. Now they are on file with our own information on the events of the day. And Mary Turner is behind bars as we speak."

"But . . . but my files were encrypted and . . ." blurted Eric.

Michael pointed to his clearance tag, raising his eyebrows.

"This is GCHQ Eric. We are the best in the business . . . however, there is another little matter that I will talk to you about later. You may be able to help us solve a little puzzle, to your liking I think. A cryptic drawing and some words . . . but only after we have finished this part first, what with this gathering of kindred spirits."

Eric looked very important and even a little embarrassed.

"Anyway, you're all free to go after we work out some security for you and your families. I will let you see Ruby in a moment. It's been a very demanding twenty four hours for her and she needs to rest before I can explain more about what has happened," continued Michael.

"Is it something I can see now? . . . I mean the puzzle . . . you know, so that I can prepare myself mentally," gushed Eric.

Harry interrupted Michael before he could make a sound.

"Aye yer daft cat . . . you go and see my Ruby right now and tell her that you love her. She'll be needing to know that first, afore you go out and play with some snakes and ladders game lad."

"You know, I told Ruby that we have to change her name just now because she has had such public exposure . . . and she came up with Scarlett. Now I ask you . . . ," sighed Michael with a frown.

Michael laughed and left the room, nodding to Harry on the way out, leaving the door open and having a quiet word with the security officer.

"And what are you going to call me?" shouted Eric.

"We will call you . . . Eric!" Michael replied sternly.

Eric looked at Harry Peters who was shaking his head slowly and preparing to launch into one of his verbal shakedowns.

"But, how do you know him?" jumped in Eric, "How do you know Mister Whitehall there?"

Harry's expression changed to sadness as he reached out to put his hand on Eric's shoulder.

> "Don't ask me Eric . . . it was such a long time ago lad. Now go in and see Ruby before I do. I want to thank my mates here personally and phone your dad," replied Harry softly.

> "Tell dad I'll call him soon," said Eric quietly, "and thank you all for rallying at such short notice. You are all legends."

> "That's Legionnaires laddie!" corrected 'Kippo' firmly.

Eric's image of them looking so proud and defiant would remain in his thoughts forever. It was the turning point in deciding that it was time to toughen up. They would not be around to look after Ruby forever.

While the reunion with Ruby was a quiet affair compared to the last time she had escaped death, it was apparent to everyone there that this new phase of an old problem was just the beginning. Someone was trying to exact revenge on them all.

Ruby had a difficult time explaining to her mum that she was not an underworld assassin and why she could not come home immediately. A mention of mistaken identity calmed her down.

Ilya Kasparov had been the first strike on some new elimination list, where Ruby was to have been despatched on the same night but had avoided being killed by the Russians, after being set up by Mary Turner. Ruby was not the only one worried about this. At least that path had closed, although with Michael mentioning double agents at work, it was impossible to know if there were any more moles to uncover.

All the while, forensics were combing through Ruby's confiscated car for any more evidence as to the identity of anyone else who had been near the car. That is, other than Mary

Turner, the same woman who wanted to end Ruby's career and had sent her home drunk in a taxi by herself.

GCHQ had quickly acknowledged that it was the same woman who appeared in Eric's video clips, taking Ruby's car and returning it damaged after Kasparov had been run over whilst Ruby slept.

The MI6 agent who had spiked Ruby's drink had been assigned to wait outside her unit but he had later been told to leave, by someone higher up the line. This is where MI6 had lost control to another mole in the works.

As Mary was being interrogated, along with that senior accomplice, their homes and those of close friends were being torn apart in the search for more evidence. Ruby wondered just how do you trust your colleagues, when all trust for your own organisation has been lost.

They granted Eric leave from his defence job to stay with Ruby and Harry Peters in a unit in Liverpool, with the perimeter and entrance to the building placed on full security alert by both MI5 and MI6. Ruby felt safe living with her dad because he also had a firearm – which he insisted was only for defence.

Eric was even safer, as he had both Ruby and Harry, and a whole platoon of legendary ex-Legionnaires readily at call. He also had the puzzle that Davis had given to Ruby, to keep his mind busy, displaying it out on the table top, alternating between staring at it and walking around it, much to the annoyance of Ruby and old Harry.

"Look Ruby. Look carefully at the puzzle," he would say.

His aching leg was an excellent feedback system to curtail any repetition.

Roger Davis' Puzzle:

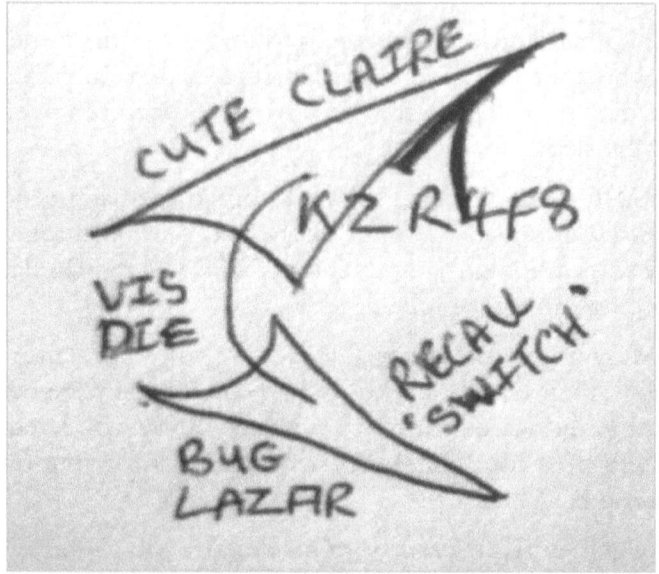

# Wake-up Call

An entire week had gone by without incident since Ilya Kasparov had been murdered on a London Street.

Eric kissed Ruby through the window of his BMW and waved goodbye to Harry who was setting off to work from his Liverpool office. Harry's sturdy old Land Rover was beginning to blow a bit of smoke but he had become too attached to it to let it go and he was a little too frugal with his money.

Ruby's intention was to rest inside for a few days before returning to the unit in London to collect her things. Although it was getting a makeover after being 'rearranged' by forensics, Eric had told her to find somewhere else because it was now probably full of bugging devices.

It was hard for her to understand why they had been so thorough. The whole exercise was to show the Russians that MI6 were doing something immediately after Kasparov was assassinated and were on top of the situation. She thought that they were only after her diamonds or they were hoping to find more evidence, leading them to the list of double agents. She suspected that her new employer was taking full advantage of that premise in order to look into all her personal items and those of Eric, for anything that may be of use to them in the future.

Eric was the biggest threat to her security clearance because he was so absorbed with his project work that he often branched out on a tangent to examine anything else that caught his eye. She had to constantly watch what he did and who he was seeing, as he would often get himself into some of the most compromising situations.

The latest example was with that weird geometric puzzle given to him by Michael to test his skills and pray on his narcissism. The origin of the puzzle was in the letter that Davis had put away for Ruby, knowing that Eric would solve it eventually . . . but it had consumed his mind for days. In fact, Ruby and Harry were getting rather tired of his perplexing theories, which came and went, as did the food and beer in Harry's fridge.

Ruby's thoughts were not idle either as she passed time at Harry's Liverpool unit. At the back of her mind was the realisation that she had not seen the contents of that envelope before MI6 had opened it. Was it really the same letter, she thought. Then there was that unusual event of Michael seconding her to work with him. Mr Whitehall! . . . The one she had told previously, that he and his entire Whitehall elite should be imprisoned, the same as with the 'Cigar Club' members.

Then there was the question of why would he want to have Eric join GCHQ. He had not even filled out the primary application form or had any specialised testing, or had run it by her as an employee of MI6 . . . and she was his girlfriend.

Roger Davis had tried to impress upon her the devious ways of the organisation and the dark world in which it operated. At times like that, she knew he really cared about her. Like the time he asked to see the four diamonds given to her by

Tan Ming Jie, senior negotiator at the Chinese Embassy and Tian's father. The premise was that the diamonds required an audit to record their unique identification - the laser inscribed codes, which could identify them should they be stolen.

That day, Ruby had agreed to meet him at the Morpeth Arms, a nice public place where they would not be overly disturbed. She was not in any doubt that the future sale of the diamonds was still her only chance of escaping from her existing life, should things become too unbearable.

"Now then, let me have a look at those stones you have there. I'll match it to the serial numbers that I have on my list. Mister Tan apologises for the inconvenience but he has the other diamonds and needs to insure them. The 'company' want to know that all the diamonds are registered. Do you have them with you?" asked Davis, coming straight to the point.

Ruby reached into her bag and opened her boxed-set of four sparkling diamonds, sliding it over to Davis who placed them directly in front of him in plain view of Ruby. Davis picked up each one and examined them closely with his eyepiece, carefully writing down and murmuring the digital code for each one. He was waiting for his accomplice.

A drink waiter came over to their table from her left side and gave her a particularly nice lingering smile. He gave the impression that he knew her or wanted to know her. She did not notice the trace of a smirk on Davis's face.

"May I get you a nice cool drink Miss?" oozed the waiter.

"No thank you. I am not staying," she replied, smiling back, wide-eyed.

She then noticed that he was wearing a badge on his lapel with 'MY6' in big letters. Surely, this was not a coincidence to be so like MI6?

"And you Mister Davis, your usual?" continued the waiter.

"Aye I'll have the usual and a packet of plain crisps."

Davis closed the box and pushed it towards her. Ruby looked back at Davis and the box, which she now had firmly in both hands. She opened it suspiciously to ensure that the diamonds were still there. Davis pretended not to notice.

"I hope to see you again soon Ruby, to let you in on a bit of a secret of mine," said Davis in a loud voice.

She put the box back into her handbag, stood up to walk away and looked amused.

"Surely, you don't have any secrets that I should know about, given your position and all that."

She stopped to look down at him, sitting quietly relaxed.

Davis looked at her the same way as when they had first met. It was those intermittent fleeting glances whilst looking straight ahead that invited her curiosity.

"So what was the code on the waiter's lapel badge?" he asked sharply.

"MY6 . . . is it important?" she replied carefully.

"Only in the fact that you looked away from me to look at that eager waiter, and took a second to evaluate the badge on his lapel. Away from your valuable diamonds for at least for two seconds. Enough time for me to put another such badge underneath those diamonds, for you to 'well remember' this day and I mean remember this day well Ruby. I could have done so much more in only one second. Remember that the word 'Switch' is similar to Swiss. It will mean much more to you in the future as a diagram. Swiss, Ruby Peters . . . Switch is Swiss. As in, I do like to be beside the seaside."

She always carried that lapel badge with her as a reminder and many time times tried to figure out just what Swiss had to do with him putting the MY6 badge under the diamonds or with that phrase about the seaside. As Ruby was remembering that day, her phone rang. She checked the header on the display. It was Eric . . . again.

"Eric. Don't you dare tell me another thing about that stupid puzzle or I'll have to come up there and sew your mouth up with your shoelaces," she said jokingly.

As usual, Eric was excited and could not wait to gush his latest findings past her, so fast in fact that Ruby took a while to understand him.

"It's on the diamonds Ruby. The list is on the diamonds. I worked it out. The coded words mean the four C's of a diamond, cut; clarity; colour; carat; the wavelength of a laser and 'vis' for face . . . it all works out. The list is engraved on the face of your diamonds."

Ruby connected what she had been thinking earlier about Davis and the checking of serial numbers with this new information . . . and it sounded incredibly like the solution that only Davis would have put together.

"Wow Eric. I think you have it at last. Don't tell anybody, do you hear? Nobody at all! That information is explosive enough to put both our families at risk. Wait until we meet up again . . . and do **not** write anything down. Promise me?" demanded Ruby.

"Yeah OK, I'll keep it quiet until I see you," he moaned.

Another call came in immediately. She looked at the call header. It was Eric's mother in Dogbol. Milly still ran the Mayfair Mews Hotel with dad, Robbie who now operated a more upmarket taxi service since he inherited that black

Bentley, given to him as the spoils of his encounter with the 'Cigar Club'.

"I'll call you later Eric. I've got your mum on the phone. She probably wants me to go and see her. Bye."

Ruby switched over calls.

"Hi Milly . . . what's happening in . . . ?"

"Ruby . . . Ruby dear come home . . . please come home. Robbie has been involved in a serious accident at the airport love. Angie has just called me to say there was an almighty explosion . . . it was the Bentley . . . it's been blown up. Oh, Ruby . . . I don't know what to do . . . I . . ."

"Stay where you are Milly. I'll come home right now and let Eric know . . . and I'll try and find out what's happening. Is Robbie hurt? Is he alright?"

There was a silence. She was crying and someone was knocking at her door with vigour.

At the same time, Ruby's communicator sprang into action with an encoded text.

"Robbie Johnson is OK. Explosion of his car at Doulton Airport. We are sending transport to pick you and Eric up. Security is around the hotel where your mother is also."

Ruby was relieved but shaken. Was it another attack on someone who is on an assassin's list? She acknowledged receipt of the message and got back to Milly.

"Robbie's OK mum, he is OK. Just hang in there. The knocking at the door is our own security and they're bringing my mum around as well. Just relax and wait until I get home."

There was just one thought on Ruby's mind. This new murderous action was now in her hometown . . . and was now targeting her family. She decided not to tell Eric yet, until she had all the facts.

Deciding not to engage with all the official drama and red tape from her plodding work colleagues, she started to pack a few items to take with her so that she could do something immediately. Waiting for a chance, she jumped out of the window into the shadows, avoiding the security patrol walking around the unit. A wise decision, as they had not noticed her leaving. These very same guards would not have seen a maniacal assassin coming for her either she thought.

When the timing was right, she ran down to the end of the alley and carefully eased herself out into the street. A firm hand grabbed her shoulder forcibly causing her to freeze.

"You took your time girl. Get in."

It was Tian. There was plenty of time for catch-up and sorrowful explanations on the trip back to Doulton. They were alike in so many ways.

Doulton Airport was in lockdown with the police, ambulances and fire crews blocking all entrances and exits. A police SWAT team carrying machine guns were searching every car and scanning people's faces for any further threats, while airport security directed the crowds to a safe muster point, away from where the explosion had taken places.

There was not much left of the parking bay where the Bentley had been. Although it was a quiet time of the day, at least five people had died in the explosion, with another eight attended by distraught ambulance crews. The police had immediately cordoned off the 'ground zero' area in anticipation of the arrival of the forensics team and the coroner.

A normally happy and friendly Angie had found Robbie bleeding on the ground, behind the massive windows immediately next to the explosion site. He had been flung to the ground by the shock wave but had received only minor injuries and some flash burns. The buckled security glass had caved in and partially melted from the ensuing fireball.

> "Are you alright Robbie? What on Earth is going on here? Why . . . that's your car outside! Why would anyone target you? Let's get you some help to see that you are OK."

Robbie stared at his crumpled wreck of a car with jagged metal surroundings, blown out components and missing bodywork. He quickly recovered his thoughts, grabbed Angie's arm and begged her to take him back to Dogbol.

> "Quick Angie, let's go. Get me out of here. I'm fine lassie . . . but I need to make sure that Milly is protected. This is too close to home."

Angie understood alright. She had not forgotten the bloodbath outside Ruby's house when Robbie was shot. He was lucky. Five others had lost their lives.

They got out of the terminal just in time before the installation of more barricades by airport staff and as more police arrived. They manoeuvred around the police lines and walked calmly over to the taxi feeder-bay, which was across from the terminal building. Angie had parked there whilst she was waiting for the next flight – a normally quiet time in her busy day, to enjoy some lunch and a chat with the other cabbies.

Robbie ignored all the comments directed at him from the other drivers all eager to know more about what was happening, directing Angie from the feeder, to the little-used perimeter dirt-track that led onto the highway roundabout.

He urgently phoned the Mayfair and was surprised to hear a man's voice. Panic set in.

> "Who's that? Where is my Milly? Where is she?"

There was a small delay. His mind began to drift back to his past. He wondered if he should phone Harry Peters and the lads from his legionnaire days. Was all this related he thought?

> "This is the Mayfair Mews . . . C.I. err, Chief Inspector Don Richards from the Doulton Police here . . . may I have your name and number and the hotel will call you back. It is temporarily closed because of a situation at the Doulton Airport."

Robbie breathed deeply.

> "Aye this is Robbie Johnson here Chief Inspector. I'm Milly's husband, owner of the Mayfair. Is she Ok, my Milly?"

> "Oh, Mr Johnson, yes your wife Milly is under our protection, as is Mrs Peter's, Ruby's mother . . . uh, please call me Don.

> "That's a relief just to know they are safe. It is as if we are never getting any closure from these goings on. Can I speak with Milly?"

Before the C.I. had time to look around, Milly had grabbed the phone on hearing his name.

> "Robbie, are you alright? I heard about the explosion at the airport and someone told me that it was your car that was the target."

> "Aye lass, it was my 'Roller' alright. But I'm OK and look . . . I want you to go into police protection, you and Debra. I want you all to be safe while this problem gets fixed, once and for all. The same goes for our Eric and Ruby. We can't just keep waiting for more things to happen Milly. It needs to be sorted," replied Robbie forcibly.

There was a delay as the C.I. took back the phone from Milly who was still shaking.

"Look, Mister Johnson . . . everything is being taken care of at this end. I have instructions to move your wife and Mrs Peters to a safe house . . . and I believe your son Eric and Ruby Peters will be arriving here soon . . . so they will all be whisked away while we survey every inch of your homes as we gather the evidence from the airport accident."

"Oh that, that was no accident Don. That was attempted murder and only a week after a friend of mine was run down by a car in London. No, this is the start of a new attack on our family and all centred on Ruby again it would seem."

Another call was coming in on Robbie's phone. It was Harry. Robbie thanked the C.I. He thought briefly about what he was going to say and then put Harry through, now prepared for bringing up old times . . . a time they had tried to forget.

"You alright Robbie? asked Harry cautiously.

"We've got problems Harry. First it was Kasparov and someone trying to frame your Ruby and now this. I'm still not sure whether it is to do with Roger Davis and his bloody surveillance debacle . . . or you know? We do have some things that may have caught up with us . . . finally," replied Robbie quietly.

Harry thought as much.

"I saw an old acquaintance at GCHQ the other day Robbie - a familiar gent in a suit in an interview office. Then it dawned on me. Time doesn't dim the memory of recognising our old pal Mike Miller. He gave Eric some sort of puzzle thing to work out too . . . and mentioned something about double agents. Who knows what he is up to? It sounds a bit queer coming from GCHQ and with your Eric being only a nineteen year old electronics graduate."

Robbie tried to match the news with what had happened.

"We need to talk Harry. We need us all to talk about the current situation and where we went wrong in the handover . . . you know . . . in Bosnia. I find it strange that MI6 were involved in trying to destroy our Ruby. Now you say Mike Miller is in GCHQ these days. They didn't protect Davis or Kasparov did they? Now I wonder why that would be."

"Aye, I agree mate. We have a volatile situation here with a lot of missing gaps in what we know and where this person or persons are operating from. They look to have no fear in eliminating a select group of people. We need to know . . . and sort it . . . like on one of our missions Robbie."

"Yes, that's right. The mission is everything. We complete it or die eh, Harry, but this time because our families are involved. We need to destroy these bastards. Aye, we need our families to be taken out of this situation until it is over," agreed Robbie.

There was a moment of reflection.

"See you at the Mayfair later. Eric and Ruby are on their way. There's more to be said in private," finished Harry abruptly.

Aye, alright then . . . you know I'm thinking that Ruby was set up and framed for Kasparov's death just to get back at you . . . at us. Poor Ilya was just a pawn in all this and your car was rigged with a timing device to kill you. That would have been three eliminations in a week. Now that would take some expert knowledge and some specific skills to do all that."

The call terminated. There was much to think about.

Ten minutes later the village of Dogbol shook with a massive booming sound. Plumes of smoke billowed over the trees in the distance, down the road from the hotel. Ruby's house had exploded. It was on fire, what was left of it. Luckily, no one had been home or around the scene.

Ruby's mother had been there only minutes earlier, picked up by car to go to the Mayfair Hotel. It appeared to Robbie to have been another timing device or maybe a remotely activated device. There was no sound of a getaway vehicle.

As Robbie and Angie were approaching the Mayfair Mews from the highway, they could see the plumes of black smoke. A police car raced past them, turning off the main road towards the country lane approach to Ruby's house. At the front door of the Mayfair, people were scurrying about in a panic. Suitcases were piling up on the front door alcove.

Milly, Debra Peters and some of the guests waited for the minibus to be brought around to the front. Police and plain-clothes minders wearing gun holsters ushered them into a corner near the big oak tree.

"Milly. Milly. Stop! I'm going to take you myself up to our safe location, up in Scotland lassie. Where's Eric and Ruby?" shouted Robbie anxiously.

Milly looked at Robbie for any signs of major injury as she picked up her suitcase and ran over to Angie's cab. He was burnt and looked as though he had been dragged out of a bonfire. Robbie ran out and hugged her.

"Eric's being picked up from his work and Ruby . . . Ruby's gone. She ran away from Harry's unit and left the guards who were there to protect her," she gushed.

"Aye lass, I'm sure Ruby will be fine. She has better connections than we do . . . although I'm beginning to wonder about just how good these people are now that she was close to being framed for a murder. She can look after herself. It's Eric I worry about love . . . he's so trusting. I'm getting you to our own safe house up in

Scotland. Harry and I have got friends there who would die for their mates and the property is remote and easy to defend."

Robbie reached for Milly's bag and threw it into the cab. He picked up his phone and dialled in his code to send a message to Harry telling him to go straight to the fishing cottage.

"Now then, let's see where our Eric is . . . we need to take him with us. He's no good staying here and I want him away from Ruby. Her agency is in a different league when it comes to the type of person we are dealing with . . . whoever they are."

Robbie sent a message to Eric. After ten minutes he sent another. There was no reply. Robbie was starting to feel anxious again.

"Right then, we are off now. I'll get Harry to swing by here and pick up Eric . . . or at least to contact him and arrange for one of our lads to pick him up," offered Robbie with a smile.

Milly just wanted to get out of her hotel, now fully convinced that it would be her last visit to Dogbol. They could retire and live down south somewhere. She looked back at the hotel as they were leaving. All those years setting it up, she thought.

Harry replied that he was just forty minutes away and that he could still not contact Eric . . . but would keep trying. Apparently, he was now with MI6 security in a black Mercedes, travelling from his workplace to the Mayfair to be with them.

He was sadly mistaken. The car had been intercepted by persons unknown and was badly damaged. The driver was dead. Not only that, he had been hacked with a machete, after first being shot in the head. Eric was not located within the damaged car or anywhere near to it. The drawing that Michael had given to him was on the front passenger seat. There were no additions or notes written on it. Only Eric and Ruby knew the solution that he had worked out. Ruby had not even told Tian.

Meanwhile, Ruby and Tian were busy catching up on all the events that had happened, starting with Ilya's death and Ruby's supervisor now held for questioning over her attempted frame-up. Tian knew more about the situation but did not let on, keeping Ruby on a 'need to know' basis for Ruby's own protection and emotional wellbeing.

Suddenly a new message interrupted their talking. It was from Henry Roberts. He was the man Tian had met when he had supervised Ruby's rescue team, at Sir Rodney's mansion. Ruby was unclear if Roberts was someone she could trust.

A gut-wrenching fear overwhelmed Ruby like never before and she felt cold and clammy. Tian realised something had gone wrong and grabbed her phone from her trembling hands.

> "They've taken my Eric. His car was attacked and the driver is dead. Eric is not there . . . but his drawing is. He must have been taken . . . Oh Tian, you know that he is not up to this sort of stuff," cried Ruby.

Tian looked at Ruby, checked her mirror and swerved off the road to pull to a stop to propose their next move.

> "You need to keep all your family safe Ruby. Get your dad and Robbie to go to their private safe house. Do not trust your own people at this stage until we know more about what is going on. We haven't seen the assassin's list. Anyone could be on it."

Ruby sent a brief message to Robbie, letting him know that she was safe and would work independently, before mentioning that Eric was missing . . . and his driver had been shot.

Robbie looked at the bleak message. It was like driving into a concrete wall at high speed. He concealed its contents from Milly and Debra, but as Angie glanced over at Robbie who had tears in his eyes and a pained look of grief, she could feel his fear.

> "Hang in there Robbie. It will all get sorted out. You'll see."

She had a sad feeling that bad news had arrived about Eric. Robbie just stared ahead. He remained quiet and so did Angie. Robbie replied to Ruby that he intended to go to Scotland with both families in Angie's cab.

Ruby's thoughts turned back to Eric and how Robbie and Milly would take the bad news, knowing that their son was in grave danger or maybe already dead. At least they were all going to a safe house. It was up to Ruby now to sort out the mess and mount a rescue to save Eric.

Ruby sent a message to Henry Roberts advising him of her concerns about Eric and that she wanted to have all the forensic information from her car, Robbie's Bentley and her house bombing sent to her immediately it was available.

There was no reply. She was now unsure about who she was dealing with.

Meanwhile, Tian received an anticipated phone call from one of Ilya's Russian friends. Their embassy was keen to offer some unofficial help and to check up on some leads they were following.

> "Tian, this is Vlado. I am so sorry for hearing the news about our Ilya. He was nice man. I know you were very close. It is sad. I have to tell you that we were told by an informant. We know that Ruby did not do this. We are keeping well away from anything to do with this investigation for fear of entrapment. You know there is a list of double agents, so you must not trust MI6 with your lives. I do not think these agents work for us anymore. They act with much violence and now also to our Ilya. We do not do this."

"Oh Vlado it is very hard for me to think about how and why it happened. I think there is more to this. Can you tell me who the informant is or anything about him?"

"My people, they tell me that the informant is from one of our mercenary outfits and that he is not to be trusted. He arrived in England about three weeks ago from Bosnia. He was a military man they say, a very, very cruel man. His entire family was killed during the Bosnia war. We look for him now so we can take him back to Russia for questioning. His name is Milo Bosnich," replied Vlado, "He has recruited others to do his work."

Tian thought quietly. She knew that both Harry and Robbie had fought in the Bosnia war as Legionnaires.

"So your people are not involved in these bombings or with Eric's kidnapping or with harming Ruby, Vlado? I have to know before planning our next move."

"No. No, we are not doing these things. We must avoid international incident. Many people will blame us. Please let me know what you find out Tian."

Tian opened the glove box and handed Ruby a Glock .40 pistol.

"This was Roger's gun . . . I found it on the road outside your house. He would have wanted you to have it . . . to protect yourself. I think you will need it very soon."

Ruby looked at the gun and thought about what her father would be saying to her about using it only for defence, but in the moment, she realised that family lives were in danger. Ruby had made up her own set of rules. She reached for the gun thinking of how Eric had fired a gun twice, to protect her. He did not know that the safety catch was on. How vulnerable he was in the ways of the dark world . . . the world that was consuming her every ounce of courage and strength.

Robbie was feeling a little better, now that his family had the protection of his platoon of ex-Legionnaires. They had remained bonded for the last fifteen years, always eager to protect and mentor any of them who needed advice or a bit of muscle. The reversal of fortune had come swiftly.

Angie had already called at her house in Doulton on the way, to pick up her engineer husband Angus. He did not seem to need too much convincing to leave his work for a while, as Scotland was always their real home anyway, at least in his mind.

Eric was in grave danger and someone was coming for them all, to seek revenge.

# Forensics

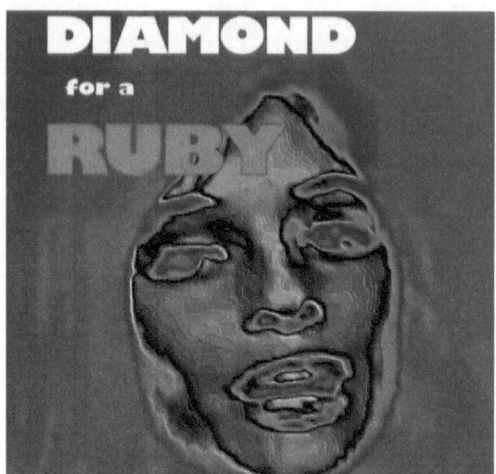

Henry Roberts had assumed command over the growing developments surrounding Ruby and her family, moving Michael Miller to one side, away from the central collection of new information. This worried Miller enough to quickly make up a list of colleagues who would be willing to keep him posted with developments, as they came to hand.

Roberts was very familiar with both Ruby and Eric, having also conducted his own research into the history of Robbie and Harry's involvement with the French Foreign Legion. For duly noted on Ruby's file, when Ruby was accepted into the intake of MI6 recruits, further intense security checks had uncovered some interesting information about her fathers' involvement with the military.

Old documents and photos identifying the two men, of course only by their Legionnaire numbers, indicated that their paths had crossed with a certain Michael Miller who now worked with MI6 in a quite senior position. Roberts was thinking about how that could be used against him.

Harry and Robbie had been young lads at the time with a sense of adventure and a yearning for travel. Their five-year stint proved to be a turning point in their lives but it was a period of failure for Roberts' junior colleague, Miller. Back then, Miller was in the British SAS based in Bosnia as well as being an MI6 operative. At the time Bosnia was a hotspot for many nationalities, each fighting their own wars superimposed on the Muslim/Christian infighting and unrest between various military factions. The United Nations was used as a cover for many of these groups, locating there as supposed peacekeepers.

The sale of arms and muscle-power was a much needed commodity back then and was being supplied by the USA, Russia, Iran and . . . the UK and others within the framework of aid.

There had been a major incident in which the Legionnaires had discovered a cache of weapons bound for the region - all high-grade and heavy-duty gear brought in and guarded by Miller and his men. One of the sides had decided that the price was too high and tried to negotiate, counting on exposing this clandestine British operation to the world if they couldn't agree with the money. With so much at stake, Miller had received orders that there would be no negotiations and that these scoundrels needed to be 'collateral damage', leaving no trace.

However, Harry, Robbie, and their platoon had acted in good faith with their own allegiance to France by stealing the weapons and ammunition for their own purposes. They had thus removed the proof that the scoundrels had required for their fraudulent case against the British.

Miller believed that the band of negotiators had stolen the cache and had no choice but to attack and kill them all, finding out later that the Legionnaires had looted their cache. He then informed the United Nations that the Legionnaires were the clandestine sellers of arms and that they had killed the locals.

As the Legionnaires had already secured a solid alibi, the British explanation of events was successfully disputed. After much diplomatic wrangling and blackmailing, the whole matter was dropped. It is an interesting fact of diplomacy that in cases like this it is best to pretend 'things' never happened at all.

Roberts shook his head and sighed when he saw the MI6 report on the matter with the dossier labelled "not for public viewing'. He wondered if Miller had forgiven them for what they had done. Maybe this was another strategic advantage for himself towards taking Miller out, possibly by pitting one against the others.

Roberts also knew Ilya Kasparov and Tian from the successful raid on Sir Rodney Applegate's mansion to rescue Ruby and Eric in earlier days. He had also met Tian's father, Jin Shi Tian the chief 'negotiator' from the Chinese Embassy. He knew a lot about everything and everyone and was now in charge of PR and loose ends.

Roberts wanted that list of double agents now and before anyone else could see it!

Roger Davis seemed to have had a close relationship with Tian on a diplomatic level leading to Davis handing over thirty-two diamonds to the Chinese Government in exchange for them carelessly spending one and a half million pounds on worthless information. It was a clear case of entrapment to the Chinese.

Roberts analysed the connections between all these people and with the latest goings on surrounding Ruby; Kasparov; the Morpeth Arms barman; Robbie's car explosion; the bombing of Ruby's house and the kidnapping of Eric. It was beginning to become obvious that 'inside information' had been leaked. Roberts needed to insulate himself from any hint of being responsible for any leaks, which would damage his remaining time at MI6.

He would have to act fast to retrieve that list first and publish it with 'amendments', and to destroy the remaining moles in the 'company' . . . leaving himself to recruit and start again. He had already arranged the kidnapping of Eric away from the others with the intention that once he had deciphered the coded message it could be destroyed . . . along with Eric.

He then imagined that Ruby would disintegrate into mental oblivion or he would have to kill her. His choice for the person to do that particular job worried him. Feliks was a drug-fuelled sociopathic maniac. Feliks was also had personal plans for further retribution on people connected with Davis. These distorted personal reasons made him a loose cannon. Feliks would have to be taken care of too . . . at a later time.

Roberts of course knew that Mary Turner and a 'senior figure' called Geoffrey Tunsdon had already been outed as double agents and were being 'interrogated' at the pleasure of Her Majesty's Government. They had not stumbled across Peter yet, who remained loyal to Roberts. He too had his time marked, for Roberts would have to make sure that Peter didn't talk about his close association with him to Miller or anyone else. It was to be a clean sweep.

Roberts had unsuccessfully tried to imply that for anyone to have brazenly killed a Russian diplomat and then try to blame it on Ruby Peters, then only 'C' could have officially ordered it. He suggested that he was only looking after the reputation of the 'company' by keeping information to himself.

Michael Miller was not convinced of this because Ruby was just a novice completing her basic training. No one would have officially sanctioned such an assignment unless they were worried about the list of double agents being decoded.

Roberts keyed in the contact number for a private conversation with one of his dangerous 'loose ends'. Mike Miller picked up.

"Ah, Henry, I was wondering when you would call. I mean, the days in Bosnia have largely been forgiven but not forgotten, within the hallowed walls of Whitehall. We don't like to be seen as fools . . . especially by our peers."

"Yes Mike. Well, we knew about that when we vetted Ruby of course, so I got to wondering if those times reflected on what we may have with us now . . . so what do you think?" replied Roberts calmly.

Michael thought it over carefully.

"No . . . No, it seems that the list of double-agents is the main key here, linked to that squiggly sketch with the bits of text from Davis. What do you think? I mean he was our best man. I would definitely put my money on that Henry, as a goer and I also think that Ruby has had enough of our cloak and dagger approach to getting Eric to decipher that damn cryptic message . . . and she has decided to go it alone, no doubt with our cantankerous Tian.

GCHQ are still working on the letter but they say that you need inside information to relate the code to real things . . . and Eric and probably Ruby, as a pair could solve what we want to know immediately. The location of that very crucial list should be our number one focus. We do not want another scenario like with that Mary Turner and old Geoffrey turning sour on their own kind. I mean, how the hell are we expected to keep anything secret if we have these damn moles entrenched in our systems?" said Michael warily.

"Yes quite. Once we get more forensics on the car that we sent for Eric and from the bomb blast at the airport, we may get a head wind. Now of course is that damn explosion at Ruby's house down in that wretched place call Dogbol. That's where we lost Davis and Barrie what's his name," said Roberts briskly.

"Barrie Barnes. Good old 'Owl'. I worked with them both at one time. Hard to replace him too of course. I'll send you all the forensics reports as they come in then," replied Michael.

"Yes that's the way old chap . . . and any news of Eric and his whereabouts? His parents must be getting pretty damn sick and tired of all these intrusions into their lives. That bloody Davis and his hiring of Ruby to spy on hotel guests! I can't tell him off now . . . and it cost him his life, over that one silly mistake."

"Two actually sir . . . he also recruited Eric," replied Michael with a sigh.

"Enough said about that. Thank you Mike, I look forward to the updates. Keep me in the loop."

The forensics team sifted through the debris alongside Robbie's Bentley – inside the car, around the bowed glass frontage of the airport. The ball-bearing projectiles spread over one hundred feet. Apart from the police, MI6 had their own military weapons expert looking for any fragments of the bomb or detonator, maybe even a timing device.

They were trying to ascertain if the bomb originated from a local cell of a known terrorist group. However, purchasing the complete bomb on the black market as a military item means that it was possible to trace it back to its origins. The audit trail could be 'extricated' by various means from the marketing people they were acquainted with.

It became immediately apparent from chemical residue, that the bomb was part of a shipment of such devices intercepted on a ship coming from Europe about one month earlier. A quick check of the ship's log showed that it had been to Singapore, the Middle East and then on to Hamburg and

Amsterdam before reaching Liverpool. The timing device and set up of the bomb showed similarities to that used by the mercenaries in Afghanistan . . . possibly of Russian or Ukraine origin. Similarly, the device used at Ruby's house looked almost identical. Pieces were beginning to fit together.

When Miller examined the forensic evidence and compared facts with what he imagined to be the key to all the events, he realised that the Kasparov murder and the bombings were separate entities. The Kasparov murder and the setup of Ruby was targeted only at Ruby, to get rid of her. Maybe Mary Turner had a strong motive there because Ruby knew too much about Davis and his findings. Kasparov had merely been the vehicle with which to frame her. They now had their culprits, which turned out to be colleagues in their own organisation.

The bombings and Eric's disappearance were targeting people around Ruby. He wondered why that would be, rather than just kidnapping Ruby. They wanted more. They wanted to get Ruby and Eric scared enough so that they would give up the list of double-agents or the means to get them . . . and now they had Eric, for his ability to crack the code . . . and he was Ruby's Achilles' heel with which to attack her emotions.

Now, it had all come down to Roger Davis and his cryptic list. Miller reluctantly contacted Roberts with his findings.

> "So there you have it. I think we need to delve into Davis's past and see where he would have got that list of agents . . . and who would know that he had it . . . and knows that he gave it to Ruby in that envelope," explained Miller cautiously.

Roberts thought over the proposition carefully himself.

> "We have left one person out of all this. Someone that was part of the Davis fiasco, the 'Cigar Club' business and the one who was part of getting those diamonds from Ruby," he mulled over aloud.

"You are thinking of Tian, the daughter of the Chinese Embassy negotiator. Yes, she played a part in all these events for sure, but we actually gave all the diamonds to them in the end anyway, as part of a diplomatic gesture. After all, we did entrap them in selling them a fictitious bundle of rubbish. It was going to be an international incident. Davis did well to pay them off."

"Gave them away? Good heavens, what were we thinking?" replied Roberts laughing.

"It was all for our peace of mind in keeping them happy with our other little ventures. Anyway, we gave back Hong Kong and Macau if you remember. Prince Charles was there. He didn't look very happy though."

They both laughed lightly.

"We do keep our word . . . sometimes. So, now then let us work on your premise and get all you know on Davis and his covert overseas missions. We can count Tian as one of us for the sake of this project then . . . but get me that list Miller. We do not want any more surprises to pop up so I want you to hand it to me personally . . . is that understood. No one else must see it . . . it may fall into the wrong hands?" continued Roberts in a more serious tone of voice.

Now at last there was a plan, but Miller was getting more suspicious of Roberts' hidden agenda. Maybe he was just being used in order to hand over the incriminating information so that the last of the moles could destroy the evidence and continue to conceal their identities.

# Betrayed

Tian watched whilst Ruby checked through her messages, both hoping that Eric had escaped from his abductors and was on his way to Dogbol again.

"Have they managed to find Eric yet?"

"No, his phone still doesn't answer and no one has made any contact with the authorities about him. I don't know where he could be and I'm beginning to worry. I just hope that they don't hurt him. I mean it's only about a trade for information, surely that's what all this is about," replied Ruby desperately.

They both knew that in their world of greed and terrorism it was not always possible to gauge how activists would react to an obviously low ranking hostage. Maybe they had just made a mistake in choosing him or realised that he was her weakest link.

Back at the forensic laboratories, the police and special operatives from the intelligence agencies were sifting through video footage from the many airport security cameras and those from petrol stations and businesses around the area. Facial Recognition software was being used to quickly find anyone already on record via their extensive database and that of Interpol. The results so far had shown several fine defaulters were going on 'holidays' and that some known drug dealers were going to and from the airport, but not actually flying anywhere.

Then there was that one nervously smiling face needing further clarification. The man in his late twenties wearing jeans, a black shirt and a brown leather jacket . . . and what looked like tennis shoes. He had a slight tan but was not of Middle Eastern appearance. He also looked a bit agitated and walked with a limp according to interviewed airport staff and passers-by. He did not catch any flights nor did he meet up with anyone else according to the video footage.

What he was doing there was anybody's guess. The grey backpack he was wearing whilst waiting for a transit bus to the town centre . . . had disappeared. It was missing just after a bus had passed in front of the parked Bentley belonging to Robbie Johnson. This man had planned the planting of the bomb like a professional.

The system brought up his name – 'Feliks Bielski', citizen of Poland, mother Katarzyna deceased, father unknown, last place of residence Kazdem Mental Asylum in Russia, escaped and dangerous'. The information was immediately analysed by MI6 for any previous connection to their intelligence work. The results were sent to Michael Miller as an update at his request. They had their man. Miller held back reporting it to Henry Roberts until he had more time to think.

Miller was on his way to Doulton and Dogbol to inspect the crime scenes set up at the airport and at Ruby's demolished house. He had seen many such bombings in his time with the British SAS in Bosnia and in Afghanistan. He wanted to see first-hand what he was up against. He took his eyes off the road in front to glance at the message header on his phone again. The name on the display hastened his reaction to stop the car. He pulled over and grabbed the phone again.

"Bielski . . . Bielski. Katarzyna Bielski! . . . Kata!" he murmured.

Everything was falling into place. His latest research had found that Kata Bielski was the woman assigned as a 'client' to Roger Davis. She had wanted to come over to the British side from her involvement with the Polish section of Russian Intelligence. Miller had already passed that information on to Henry Roberts, his senior and very few people knew about it.

According to the files, Davis was there to prepare for her transfer . . . and more importantly to secure the information that she had on British spies who were selling secrets to the Russians. Miller noted that they seemed to have formed a very close relationship after only a few weeks and that Kata was going to give him the list of double agents.

However, disaster struck one day out from her defection, as the secret police had arrested her in the middle of the night along with her son Feliks who was nineteen at the time. Davis had narrowly escaped capture by jumping from a second floor window onto the top of a parked car, then making his way to a safe house. Both Kata and Feliks were severely tortured. Kata was later found floating in the river to prove a point. Her injuries were so severe that the medical report was not made public.

Feliks had had his arms and legs broken and several fingers hacked off with a chisel before they dumped his dishevelled half-naked body into the courtyard of the local school. He was barely alive and had undergone a total mental breakdown. He ended up in the mental asylum where he spent six months under intense medical supervision. He had escaped only recently by stockpiling his medication . . . and had tortured and murdered three staff. Many remaining staff members traumatised by what they had witnessed had resigned. Some were on sick leave. It was such a savage and prolonged attack.

Davis had noted on his report that he suspected someone from MI6 had informed on her in order to shut her up and to prevent her from giving him the list of names. There was a post-note from 'C' indicating that although Davis had not obtained the list . . . it was suspected that he did in fact know its location and was possibly keeping the information to himself for future unknown use . . . maybe to act out alone.

Feliks Bielski had now entered Britain. He was on video planting the bomb at Doulton Airport. It seemed that Feliks had the same hatred as Davis for those who had betrayed him and his mother but for different reasons.

He knew that the same people had murdered Davis too. Feliks had meticulously stockpiled every newspaper report that he had been assassinated in an international murder which had appeared to him as more evidence that Davis and his mother were set up by MI6. He was still feeling for the loss of his mother and suffered much pain associated with his torture. He was now a drug addict and suffered multiple psychological problems.

Further enquiries by Feliks had revealed that Eric and Ruby were at the centre of Davis's death and he mistakenly viewed them as hostile too. Feliks had even watched Ruby attend Davis's gravesite on the same morning as the function at the Morpeth Arms. He had looked at her weeping silently, with her long-flowing hair covering up a grieving face of regret. She reminded him of his mother and he longed to touch her and bring her close to him. Feliks had started to drift in his mind with memories and hate for what had happened, but when he had looked up . . . Ruby too had gone away.

Feliks had also formed a loose alliance with other agents in Russia who had escaped the clutches of the Russian KGB and the Bosnian war and who now acted for themselves. They took the opportunity of using him for their own gain and it was they, who now communicated with their remaining contact deep within MI6. Someone high up but merely a contact codename.

From this source, Feliks had collected all the information about the Davis and 'Cigar Club' operation, including the Scarab abduction, the CIA diamond heist and the bloodletting outside Ruby's house where five people died. He was beginning to thrive on stories of carnage and suffering. His mission was to find the missing list of double agents and kill off any leads associated with him finding it. There were to be no 'loose ends'.

Although an MI6 mole under orders to prevent the list and Kata from turning up in England had turned him and his mother in, his twisted mind targeted the entire 'company'.

His 'guilt by association' had also allowed him to find the bartender who had kept the envelope from Davis, to pass on to Ruby. Mary Turner had told Roberts that she suspected some sort of transaction had taken place between the barman and Ruby. The barman's apparent unwillingness to disclose the contents of the envelope had put Feliks into an uncontrollable rage.

He had shoved the bartender into the walk-in freezer in the kitchen and after slashing at him with an array of knives and hanging up some of his limbs on meat hooks, he abandoned the bloody remains, leaving a knife protruding from the victim's eye as a calling card. When the chef had run out of steaks for the kitchen, he had opened the fridge door and had been overwhelmed with the urge to be sick.

The hotel murder was now the scene of another gruesome crime that linked Davis, Robbie, Ruby and Eric . . . adding to the perception that they were dealing with the worst kind of psychotic killer. The autopsy report was amended to 'classified until the murderer has been apprehended' but MI6 wanted it to be a classified document.

An all-points-alert was immediately sent out to all the police stations and mobile patrols, that Feliks Bielski was a deranged sociopathic assassin who must be contained but not approached until they had sufficient backup. Special Forces and a number of SWAT teams were already on standby.

'He may be armed and under the influence of drugs,' it stated in both voice and text messages.

Ruby and Tian were about three miles from Dogbol when they had received the same alert. Michael had followed up by sending her a watered down update of the official report on Feliks, saying that it looked like he was acting alone. Ruby didn't like the way Miller was dumbing her down.

She questioned her mind about where Feliks could be. Did he have Eric as a hostage? Was Eric OK? These were the questions that many wanted answered.

That came soon enough with the sending of a short message to direct to Ruby . . . from Eric's phone. Tian pulled over to the curb when she saw Ruby's face.

'Hi Sweetie, I have a brand new friend. He wants to meet you. OK my dear?' – read the SMS.

Ruby knew that Eric did not send it. She showed it to Tian and started typing frantically.

"Where shall we meet? I think I will like your new friend if he looks after you Eric," she replied.

Tian was feeling that she could do more to help Ruby and poor Eric, if he was in fact still alive. She got out of the car to phone her father at the Chinese Embassy. They had a long talk about the recent events before Tian could see that Ruby was still waiting for a reply.

She got back in the car and stroked Ruby's hair.

"We will get him back Ruby. He will be OK if we can just get to where he is being held," she said encouragingly.

Ruby waited a full fifteen minutes before the phone rang. Tian looked at her watch . . . it was exactly fifteen minutes. They both understood that this person was operating according to a tightly timed schedule and would probably become unstable if things did not go to plan.

"Hello, hello is that you Ruby?"

"Yes, it is. Where is my Eric . . . can I talk to him please? What do I call you?" she replied slowly and calmly.

There was a delay. Ruby stopped herself from talking.

"My name is Feliks. I have been watching you for quite a while Ruby . . . visiting the grave of Roger Davis . . . the Morpeth Arms . . . and what a nice family you have . . . Ruby Peters."

Ruby took a deep breath.

"Did you know Roger? Was he a friend . . . I know he didn't have a family of his own . . ."

She got cut off abruptly.

"He had a family! . . . my mother and me . . . he had a family and we were going to come to England, Ruby . . . but your people at MI6 didn't want that. No, they informed on my mother and she was taken away . . . tortured to death while I was made to watch them. They cut off her hands and broke her bones . . . and stabbed her in the eye with hot pokers . . . and then they hurt me too Ruby. They cut off my fingers and broke my limbs Ruby . . . I see it all the time in every waking moments and when I try to sleep . . . I can't," he screamed in agony, ending in a whimper.

Tian touched Ruby's hand to warn her to take things slower.

> "I am so sorry Feliks. I was not part of that. Eric was not part of that . . . we were at school . . . we were only schoolchildren. We were only sixteen years old Feliks . . . Can I speak to him . . . to my Eric? . . . He has nothing to do with any of this. He did not harm you or your mother Feliks. Let him go, please."

There was a silence. It was quiet enough to hear another voice and some moaning and crying in the background. It had to be Eric. Someone picked up the phone again.

> "They killed my mother because she had made up a list of double-agents to give to Davis . . . do you not know of this? I was told by my friends but now they are all dead too . . . and I know you have this list . . . so this is what I want from you . . . to expose them all. You are now one of them Ruby . . . and I will take away that which is dear to you . . . like I lost my mother. You will feel my pain too Ruby," continued Feliks with rising tension.

There was shouting in the background.

> "Stay away Ruby . . . he will kill us all!" It was Eric.

What followed was a combination of screams and noises resembling a car crash, before complete silence.

> "What's going on? What are you doing to Eric? I will not help you if you hurt him . . . now where are you, so we can talk?" shouted Ruby in anger.

There was breathing and a deep sigh.

> "I am at your hotel Ruby. I am in the wine cellar . . . with Eric. If you don't come alone, I will kill him in a most painful way . . . there's no reason to talk with him anymore . . . he has no ears to hear you with . . . what a

nice world that must be Ruby . . . imagine the stillness and quiet, for resting and sleeping . . ."

"Stop right there Feliks. Eric does not have the list. I have the list. I am the one you want. Do not hurt him!"

"Ah, but Eric has been kind enough to decipher that little note from dear Roger . . . you know the one with the triangles and funny shapes and those words Let me read them again . . . **CLAIRE, CUTE, DIE, BUG, LAZAR** and **VIS**. Oh how clever was our Roger Davis and now it seems your lovely Eric also, for solving the puzzle. I doubt that GCHQ have any idea at all . . . so bring your diamonds to me Ruby!" replied Feliks raising his voice.

"Why do you want the diamonds? You have decoded the letter already haven't you?" said Ruby hurriedly to gain some time.

"Because the puzzle on the letter shows that the list is engraved on the face of those diamonds my dear, as you well know . . . and I want to have the list as well as those pretty diamonds. If you want to spare young Eric any more pain . . . or loss of his sight for instance, so he can never see you again," replied Feliks slowly.

He was playing with her and she did not have the diamonds with her and was not much interested in the riddle at all. Eric was more important than information. She looked at Tian with a grimace hiding her pain to indicate that she wanted some help.

"My father is talking with Michael Miller at MI6 and we are covered to go in there and get this bastard . . . and get Eric out," whispered Tian.

Ruby quickly agreed with a nod. They would storm the room and take this man down. Time was of the essence and it was probable that Eric already had extensive injuries. The problem was that Eric would be despatched in an instant if

Feliks was forced to escape or was allowed any time to dwell on matters that were real or imaginary.

> "I will be there in ten minutes Feliks. Make sure that Eric is able and ready to leave with me . . . once I give you the diamonds."

There was no answer.

"Feliks . . . Feliks!" screamed Ruby.

The police had cordoned off the hotel and both Ruby and Tian could not understand how Feliks was hiding there amongst all the security. Surely all the rooms would have been double-checked and no one allowed to enter or leave this restricted area. He must have been waiting there for some time.

Ruby jumped out of the car and raced towards the main entrance where she was stopped by security. Flashing her MI6 identity, she quickly resumed her run towards the wine cellar.

Tian was also stopped by the police and told to leave, even after telling them of Ruby's plans. So reluctantly she made her way back to sit in the car. They had their orders. However, Tian soon disappeared from around the car, diving through an open window at the rear of the building.

Ruby flew down the stairs and pushed open the wine cellar door with an arm outstretched bearing the Glock pistol. There was Henry Roberts, with gun in hand . . . and her Eric crumpled up on the ground. His bloody torso and various body parts were left strewn around the room as if the murderer had been in a wild frenzy. There was a knife protruding from his eye.

A shockwave of horror and sudden panic rushed through Ruby's body to the point of total incapacitation. Unable to scream her pain, she sank to her knees with her eyes closed and her arms tightly wrapped around her head.

Roberts was struggling himself but grabbed her arm and tried to lift her gently from the frozen position of her nightmare. The grisly sight and putrid smell of warm body fluids had put Ruby into total shock and Roberts was gasping for air.

"He'd already gone Ruby. I got here too late."

Tian rushed into the room with gun drawn and stopped abruptly as if hit by a truck on seeing what had happened.

She turned to Ruby and quickly removed her from the room, covering her nose and mouth gently. Reaching to the floor, she retrieved Ruby's gun, the one that had belonged to Davis. He would not have imagined this tragic outcome for Eric. There was no sign of Feliks. The appearance of Roberts met with a suspicious stare from Tian.

"I . . . I got a call on my mobile to meet Ruby here . . . and this is what I found. There's no sign of Feliks . . . I am so sorry Ruby that this has happened. I can't imagine what this means to you . . . I'm so sorry," rushed Roberts as he frantically spoke to his crisis coordinator for backup on his communicator.

The police descended upon them in a rush.

"Wine cellar at the Mayfair Mews . . . one down and Feliks has escaped. He could be dressed in uniform to get past all the security here. He is a frenzied killer and must be stopped immediately . . . shoot to kill . . . just shoot that bastard!" ordered Roberts angrily.

With the puzzle of the list solved, Roberts had no interest in anything except getting hold of the diamonds. He wanted that list ahead of anything else. Other lives were at stake. But Ruby wanted to know how Roberts knew so early, if he hadn't detained Feliks or spoken with Eric or Ruby about the diagram.

Several of the police who had joined them were having trouble viewing the carnage that had taken place under their watch. Roberts turned to Ruby who was still trying to cope.

> "Look . . . this is a very bad time . . . a very sad time I know . . . but we need to get those diamonds from you Ruby . . . so that all this can be settled . . . that would bring an end to all these killings . . . if you could just let me know . . . ," offered Roberts impatiently.

Tian glared at Roberts' lack of emotion. She had no proof that he was not in some way responsible for what had happened.

> "You'll get nothing here except contempt!" replied Tian angrily.

Roberts looked at the police gathered around. Their expressions echoed Tian's feelings. Tian looked back briefly as she comforted Ruby whilst leading her away back up the stairs towards a waiting ambulance. It had been on standby in case of trouble.

> "Look after her," shouted Tian to the ambulance medic and a plain-clothes officer, deciding that she should at least look for this Feliks, not knowing that the officer was the same drink-spiking agent who was at the Morpeth Arms.

There was only a small chance that Feliks would have planned to stay hidden for a long time, for even he had to eat and sleep sometime. Her mind turned to imagining all the cruel ways this animal should be tortured. Even how to dispose of his body with no care for the legal consequences or for the sanctity of his remains.

After having seen what had happened to Eric, she could only think back to her Ilya and the fractured life that they had to endure together. She loved him so much . . . after years of telling herself that it would be impossible to have such a close relationship. Their time together had ended far too soon.

That was the way of their lives for it only takes the blink of an eye, or a turn in a road, to yield to the outcome of life or a cruel death from the hand of fate.

She jumped into the car and drove away from the hotel, scouring the faces of police and locals, searching every possible exit point from the area, looking for any signs of Feliks. She soon realised that he had a good fifteen-minute start and could be anywhere, especially if he had help.

Ruby texted Miller with the news of Eric's death, the presence of Roberts and briefly explained how Eric had solved the puzzle. Miller replied that he was devastated and didn't have the words to express his feelings for Ruby's loss. As the information filtered through, many people now knew that Ruby had the key to the list of double agents and that a diamond had been the vehicle for carrying the information.

Ruby was now in extreme danger and the current focus of attention. GCHQ had finally cracked the code too now that the 'local knowledge' had been supplied by Eric. The two triangles and lambda symbol combined with the simply coded names for the four C's of diamond classification, had completed the puzzle enough for them to realise that one of the diamonds had the list etched on to its cut faces.

The very same diamonds that Ruby had briefly shown to Roger Davis, the day he had switched one of the diamonds and placed that MY6 badge under the tray before closing the box. With sleight of hand and the voice of Davis etched into permanency, his last words had been retrieved from beyond the grave by a close friend.

Ruby remembered what he had said to her that day:

"Remember that the word 'switch' is similar to Swiss . . . it will mean much more to you in the future. Swiss, Ruby Peters . . . Switch is Swiss."

Ruby had been taking care of the diamonds herself, relieving Harry of their care, knowing that he would have been in great danger . . . with her diamonds now holding the demise of double agents buried in the depths of MI6 itself.

That list could bring about many deaths or save lives depending on who got them first. The integrity of British security was at stake. Like Davis, Ruby was now wondering just who to trust with such matters, when there is a mole in the organisation . . . or many.

# Regroup

R uby awoke in a panic with fleeting images within her mind of the discovery of her Eric's violated body. She found herself searching for an escape as tears flowed down her warm cheeks. Cautiously looking around the light green, dimly lit hospital room for that familiar face, all she could see was the sadness in the eyes of her devastated family.

The young man who had changed her life through his deep love for her was gone forever. Her world had changed in one day.

Ruby's mother was holding her hand and stroked her hair gently, rhythmically. She had been crying all night but was now holding in her grief and managed a soft reassuring smile.

Robbie and Harry looked on quietly with such sad faces that their silence spoke a thousand words of despair. Robbie could not understand why his only child was now dead and his wife was suffering too great a burden for her mind to cope.

Milly had also been hospitalised and sedated following her collapse on hearing the shattering news from an uncontrollably sobbing Robbie. After a seemingly endless night watching over his distraught wife, Robbie was finally taking some time out to visit Ruby and her own distressed family.

Ruby's world was now full of despair and decay. She had almost had enough of its prolonged suffering. She was falling apart.

Then she saw Tian standing proudly at the doorway, looking at her with reassurance, like a sentinel bird watching over its flock.

How could she remain so fiercely strong after losing Ilya? She looked so composed, with that same determined look of wanting to sort things out, to intervene and protect others . . . and yet eager to exact punishment on those who had dared to harm the one she loved.

She too had suffered the loss of the love of her life.

Her Ilya would have understood the sad reflective moments of her sadness and pain, yet he would have also fortified her resolve to find the murderer, before grieving for him.

Tian knew that she would crave some private time once her ordeal was over. Such was the way her father had managed to deal with the death of his wife, when she was only six years old.

> "Fight when you must . . . but grieve when you are strong once more . . . for to remain in grief is to die twice over . . . amplifying that loss many times over, for surrounding family and friends."

Even Harry, would be repeating the Legionnaire's resolution to 'complete the mission at all cost' to Ruby. He had prepared her since childhood to look after her own wellbeing foremost, above everything else.

Ruby's fellow recruits at MI6 were also feeling her pain, hoping for her to recover soon to lead the way into upholding justice. She had given them an insight into how to remain calm in action, with a determination to survive. From hearing her talk excitedly about Tian and Ilya, they had learnt that sometimes foreign agents can work together to bring about justice. Some can even fall in love . . . for as long as it is allowed to continue.

Michael sent personal messages to Robbie and Harry. Then, thinking more about the gravity of the situation, he had phoned Robbie to talk about the things that only ex-soldiers can share with each other at times like this. They even talked a little about the messy Bosnia business. It all seemed much easier now to accept that soldiers always have to follow orders, regardless of what they thought about them.

However, spying is a different 'game'. It is meant to stop wars and terrorism from happening in the first place . . . especially when diplomacy is in such disarray and lunatics get elected by a naive and apathetic populace. The people get what they vote for but then democracy is only useful for a small population. The Ancient Greeks knew that all too well.

Information gained to counteract and destroy any thoughts of aggression from the perceived enemy is paramount. The elimination of a threat is likely to prevent future problems from arising at a much greater cost. The common enemy now hails from those with power and who lust for more, with some people assuming that they have a right to be treated better than others. So, they engage in skimming, side swapping, terrorism, corruption . . . and killing.

Henry Roberts was a case in point, being more concerned with increasing his wealth than fighting crime. Born into the elite and inheriting a high-level advantage throughout Whitehall, he could do no wrong within that honourable den of thieves. It was common knowledge that he had dealings with some rogue elements of high society, initially deemed to be 'alright' although 'rather awkward'. However, some of his friends had over-stepped the boundary of acceptance by the establishment, leading to their arrest and prosecution by example, by their peers.

Roberts countered with the fact that they had all gone to the same schools and university colleges, so it was inevitable that their business interests would sometimes overlap. Even the 'Cigar Club' defence team pointed out that its members, who were also part of the elite were merely selling false information to the enemies of Great Britain, which was of no use to them at all. In fact, it exposed the buyer's identity.

However, the prosecution successfully argued that they would not have known at the time of 'acquiring' such information, that it was in fact 'useless' and they had been paid for that information using off-shore money laundering accounts.

Michael realised it was time to regroup and sort out exactly who was reliable and who was not, before proceeding. Sharing information that could be passed on to their enemies had to be contained and handled by only those he could trust. There was a psychotic killer on the loose with a vengeance for MI6 operatives, accessing inside information. With Ruby and her family currently being his main targets, this actually gave him an advantage in picking his new team. He could safely rely on Ruby, Harry, Robbie and Tian to work with him.

There was one other person who he thought would give his life for the service . . . that was Peter Richards. Peter was his young MI5 protégé that he had sent to the Morpeth Arms to make sure that Ruby was seen to go home, then remaining there with a strong alibi. As with Ruby, Michael had seconded him to work with him directly on critical missions.

Along with a speciality in psychological profiles and database analysis techniques, Peter was also a good socialiser . . . and an amateur actor. The latter skill would prove to be an extremely valuable skill as he worked without conscience through Henry Robert's plans behind the scenes.

Michael's tip-off from an informant about Ruby being set up for a crime to discredit her and leave her open to assassination by the Russians had been spot on, but he hadn't known that Ilya was the target for a cruel assassination.

From information received from his field agents, he had been wary about dealing with certain of his work colleagues . . . including field-operative Mary Turner and section-leader Geoffrey Tunsdon. They were currently under investigation and their close friends put under surveillance.

He also had strong reservations about Henry Roberts who was now sidelining him by taking charge of the investigation. He had no proof, yet had to work under his instructions, passing on information and ideas about the unravelling situation.

The rumours about a list of double agents had been floating around the agency since Roger Davis had been ordered to transition Kata Bielski's defection to Britain. The mission had been a disaster for Davis, who later argued strongly that Kata had been sold out to the Russians, by someone within the 'company'. Her mutilated body found floating in the river was evidence to that effect.

In floundering through damage control, MI6 had refuted the suggestion that it was an inside job and blamed the Russians for acting on their own intelligence reports. Three years after the death of Davis, those rumours had resurfaced and was now being given credibility again, by the arrival of Kata's son, Feliks Bielski and his savage lust for revenge.

It was now common knowledge that the list of agents was etched onto Ruby's four diamonds which she had taken back into her own safekeeping. It was a secret no more.

Michael made a quick phone call to confirm that Harry and Robbie were at the hospital. The elusive Tian had also been there but her whereabouts were now unknown. She was like some formless creature that patrolled the battlefield, exacting revenge on her enemies before caring for the fallen and suffering, only to disappear once more into the shadows.

Michael decided to give Robbie another call to sort through some of the details of what had happened. He answered immediately with a sharp reply.

"Robbie here!"

"Mike here Robbie. I know you are all having the worst time at the moment . . . but there are things that need to be done without wasting any time. And you and Harry and Tian are the only people I can rely on. We have a killer on the loose looking for your family and related to that, we have the matter of that list of double agents. The Russians and even some people within my organisation will stop at nothing to get their hands on it. It is a double-edged problem affecting us all."

Robbie thought about the last time they had spoken.

"Aye Mike, you'll be wanting to see the diamonds then I presume, to get your list sorted first. Well, I can do better than that because Harry used an eyeglass to look at the laser-etched writing after Ruby told him where to look. He wrote down the four names . . . they seem to be nicknames. We should meet in person. I'm not saying anything over the phone. Your moles may be passing on information about our movements to Feliks," offered Robbie thoughtfully.

"I can't thank you enough Robbie. Four names? Good heavens man . . . as many as that? Removing them from the agency will make our job of catching Feliks much easier. He would have required some internal help in getting over here and knowing as much as he does. We have a profile on him . . . not very good reading Robbie. He has multiple psychological problems that require him to be restrained and on medication . . . but it seems he would rather be roaming our streets on ICE and can stay awake for days at a time. He is totally unpredictable . . . quite mad it seems. He needs to be . . . despatched!"

"Aye I can think of a better term. I'm with Ruby and Harry at the moment. Can you meet me here in twenty minutes Mike?"

"I'll be there Robbie . . . alone . . . No wait. I'll bring someone who actually saved Ruby from being killed on the night of her drink-spiking . . . Peter Richards. He's a psychologist too and my best operative."

Robbie thought about what Mike had inferred.

"How do you reckon that then. Surely it was Eric with his electronics that saved her . . . on those videos," asked Robbie cautiously.

"Ah, Robbie, Eric's videos proved the point but if it wasn't for her drink getting spiked at the pub, keeping her at home out of harm's way, then the Russians would have exacted revenge on her immediately. The plan was to make it look like Ruby had run over Ilya. That was the whole plot Robbie. Getting both Ilya and Ruby. The two of them in the one night."

"But who?" interrupted Robbie.

"Unfortunately it was some of our own Robbie. Mary Turner you already know . . . she was in Davis's team . . . and the other was a senior officer . . . I can't tell you his name yet."

Robbie remembered Mary from the day he took a bullet in the shoulder, that day Davis died and she had visited the hospital with Eric and Ruby.

"The initial motive was to get the double-agents list from Ruby by eliminating all those involved in the

'Cigar Club' mission, thus pinning the blame back on their remaining members. But we now have Feliks coming into the picture to join them, with a different angle. His mother was murdered in a botched MI6 defection with that same list being the bargaining chip.

Now of course he is totally psychotic and appears to want to hurt as many MI6 agents as possible . . . especially Ruby . . . Davis's friend and someone that he feels he needs to destroy, including her family.

There's also the matter of finding out just what part these damn double-agents are playing in all this and who the hell they are working for," continued Mike angrily.

Robbie was shaking his head as he thought about the ramifications.

"I'll see you in twenty Mike. My family are at risk. I will only talk with you from now on . . . I can't trust anyone else, that's for sure."

"Right then, twenty minutes," replied Mike briskly.

# Profiling

Doulton Hospital was on full alert for any intruders trying to get to the fourth floor security wards where both Ruby and Milly were recovering from the shock of Eric's tortuous death.

MI5 had taken control of the hospital perimeter with armed personnel and two snipers, with the fourth floor guarded by MI6 agents who were also patrolling the surrounding corridors and lift wells. Police command were monitoring the hospital security cameras using facial recognition software superimposed over the data stream.

The whereabouts of Feliks, charged up with murderous thoughts and the almost expected attempt by the Russians to obtain the list of double agents, had to be handled as one issue, with orders of 'shoot to kill' endorsed by 'C' himself.

Robbie and Harry had also arranged for some of their ex-Legionnaires to be on stand-by within the hospital with the understanding that they were only there to pass on information to Robbie and Harry. Most of them stationed themselves around the café, overlooking the central lift shaft. Trust in the 'company' had reached rock bottom for the old platoon. Michael Miller was the only link they could trust.

Mike and Peter Richards arrived directly to the secured ambulance bay and took the private lift up to the fourth floor. Mike was satisfied that it was a good enough check on the security personnel. He watched them stop and verify the credentials of everyone working on and around the floor.

Robbie and Harry were sitting next to Ruby's bed whilst Debra looked after Milly in another private room. Ruby had been mildly sedated but was already starting to feel like she was gaining control of her physical and emotional self again.

"Hi there, I'm so sorry Ruby. I hope you're feeling much better now. We are all working around the clock to get things sorted," said Mike quietly before seeing the downcast Robbie.

"I'm so sorry about Eric, Robbie. He was the real hero in all this and I just can't explain or have the right words to describe how much we will all miss him and his constant protective efforts to look after Ruby," added Mike.

Ruby looked at Mike with raised eyebrows. So, this is what he was like normally, rather than that bland sloth-like creature that conducts interviews slowly, in fits and starts. He actually has emotions, feelings and sometimes cares about others.

"I'm ready to get back to my job . . . boss," she replied quietly.

Then she noticed the young man standing next to him and after confirming her suspicions, she leaped out of her bed and thrust her hands towards his throat, screaming at him.

"Whoa, steady on there Ruby! He's on our side. This is Peter, my profiler," shouted an alarmed Mike.

Harry and Robbie had immediately assumed a defensive pose and were ready to take both Mike and Peter out. Harry had pointed his Glock .40 at Mike's head, the moment Peter had deflected Ruby's arms and had turned her around to face Harry.

> "Ok everyone. Let's calm down. Harry put the gun down," eased Robbie, waving his hand slowly.

> "He's the bastard who drugged me at the hotel . . . the start of all this mess," cried Ruby, struggling to break free.

> "No Ruby . . . I know the truth to this . . . he drugged you to keep you home . . . to save you from being killed by the Russians . . . for supposedly killing Ilya. He was under orders. That was the original plan for you and Ilya. Back off and calm down," interjected Harry.

Ruby stopped fighting. Peter let her go but was soon on the receiving end of a solid kick to the shin, as was her way with frustration and annoyance.

> "Ruby . . . Stop that! He's one of us," added Robbie hastily.

Peter rubbed his shin and looked at Ruby in the same way that Eric had done . . . sort of like a child after being punished.

> "Ruby this is Peter Richards . . . and Peter, well you two have met before over drinks I think we have established. This is Ruby," offered Mike with a hesitant smile.

Ruby looked as if she wanted to do some more collateral damage, but something about Peter's expression made her come to her senses. Maybe it was his bland expression. It often puzzled her that someone could actually look like a person to trust with your life. However, Peter was not one of these.

"Ruby, I'm sorry for spiking your drink but we had been advised what was going to happen last minute and it was my suggestion that you should stay at home with a solid alibi . . . otherwise we wouldn't be talking now. I had to convince Mike after I had done it, that it was your only chance to be off the streets. I got reprimanded for it . . . big time," said Peter.

"Well I for one can't thank you enough for breaking protocol my lad. You saved my daughter from a Russian hit. They don't play around," replied Harry before Ruby could abuse him again.

Ruby could not believe that Peter was being made out to be a hero in all this. After all, it was her Eric who had made sure that her unit was secure with cameras and recordings . . . and he had left her with his hairgrip transmitter. Now, Eric was being forgotten in favour of this wild card of an obnoxious agent.

After everyone felt more comfortable with being able to talk freely about the situation, Ruby sat back on her bed glaring at Peter. She was still a bit woozy, but able to suppress her odd sense of balance. Enough to rationalise what was going on.

Peter went out to get everyone a coffee and on returning emphasised a slight limp which made Ruby smile briefly. Mike was ready to get started with his address to the group.

"Now then, I will be fully in charge of our operations together until we have dealt with Feliks and have acted on that list of double-agents, to remove any reliance on other members of my agency. Peter is a psychologist with MI5 and has the distinction of being both a field operator and also a profiler. Peter . . . perhaps you can explain what you do and how we can use your expertise to trap Feliks with minimal risk. Oh, and I'll have a quick look at the list which Robbie has obtained from the diamonds to see if we can work out who the moles are in my organisation," said Mike.

Robbie pulled out the list from his back pocket and handed it to Mike.

> "It was Harry who had the diamonds examined for this list after talking with Ruby and he gave it to me for safekeeping," said Robbie quickly to acknowledge Harry's efforts.

> "And Eric was the one who decoded it," snapped Ruby.

Peter began talking about the type of character that they were looking for. The character profile which matched the actions and thinking of Feliks Bielski.

> "Thank you Mike, I'll start off by saying that the person we are looking for is a very sick person who witnessed his mother being brutally tortured and murdered before they turned on him . . . breaking his bones and . . . well I won't dwell on that.

> Anyway, he is not a psychopath. No, but he is psychotic and suffers from quite a few problems including paranoid schizophrenia. He has psychotic episodes from not taking his medication, although he now takes ICE, which is a bad development. So, after all the shock and trauma of the physical violence carried out on him and his mother, he then found out that Davis, who had promised to take them both to the UK . . . was part of a deliberate betrayal. Someone at MI6 had informed the Russians about the existence of the double-agents list and that his mother was passing it on to MI6 in exchange for a new life for her and her son.

> He viewed Davis as being like a substitute father figure, looking after their family and helping them to escape to a new life together. Then he sees the article about Davis's death in the newspapers and it sets him off. He readily finds people who want to exploit his paranoia,

illusions, delusions, voices in his head, lack of sleep and his addiction to drugs.

I forgot to tell you that he broke out of a mental asylum after killing three staff. Now he has access to someone in MI6 who is supplying him with information about Ruby and all those associated with the 'Cigar Club' dramas. So there you have it . . . our Feliks . . . a danger to himself and to all those who make him feel threatened. I'm afraid he looks like a hopeless case in my view and must be incarcerated for life . . . or destroyed," concluded Peter with a hint of sympathy.

"I would exterminate that animal with my bare hands. He is just an evil murderer with no remorse," cried Ruby in anger.

"He has phenomenal strength too Ruby. I forgot to mention that . . . and he feels no pain or remorse during or after his attacks. That is until many hours later when he becomes depressed," added Peter looking at Ruby's look of pure hatred for Feliks.

Whilst occasionally staring at Ruby during his rundown of past events, it was enough to make her feel a little uncomfortable about Peter's empathy for this criminal. She began to think back over the day when she had her drink spiked. Then, back to her last cemetery visit, but no, not on that particular day . . . it was well before that. In fact, it was soon after Davis's funeral. She had just made another startling connection in her busy mind. Ruby sprang up from her bed in a rage, taking everyone by surprise. It looked like she was going to attack Peter again.

"It was you! . . . You! . . . You were the one stalking me . . . at the cemetery . . . every month after the burial for about a year. I felt your presence and I once saw your outline. It was you! I can see it, by the way you are standing, your profile against the lighting," she blurted.

Mike stood up with the intention of denying it whilst Harry thought that she was slipping back into delirium and stopped her from jumping off the bed again. Peter however, looked at her with the same look that she imagined she saw in the shadows. It was a hollow, haunting look of sadness.

"Yes . . . that was me. I had been watching you on some of your earlier visits to the cemetery . . . just to see if he had anyone at all who cared about him . . . but definitely not later on I can assure you Ruby," offered Peter before being interrupted.

"Peter? Did you do that Peter, and on whose authority? It certainly wasn't mine . . . and you didn't bother to tell me of your surveillance of Ruby!" shouted Mike angrily, realising that there was something else he didn't know about his organisation and colleagues.

Harry and Robbie looked at Peter very suspiciously.

"You'd better explain lad . . . or we'll have to detain you as a suspect. You could be the mole in the 'company'," said Robbie slowly, moving towards him.

All eyes were on Peter. Mike was ready to shoot him if he moved to escape. Harry's hand had worked its way down to where he kept the Glock .40.

Ruby was more confused and felt threatened realising that she had not seen any of this previously. The words of the kind, friendly barman came back to haunt her about trusting her colleagues. He had suffered a violent attack for his association with Davis and Ruby. He was dead.

"My family background was my reason Mike, Harry, Ruby . . . my family is the reason that I found myself wanting to get to know you Ruby. You knew my father for what he really was . . . and in return he protected you . . . and I wanted to know why, so that I could work it into my memory of what he really must have been like," answered Peter, looking at Ruby and then Harry.

"What are you talking about man?" asked Harry.

Peter walked towards the window and turned around.

"You visited my father every month Ruby . . . you showed your feelings for the man who thought he had no life, or anyone who cared. You share my admiration for him . . . for the father I never knew I had until he was gone forever," he said, holding back his grief.

Ruby looked at him in disbelief.

"You . . . are Roger Davis's son?" she asked wide-eyed.

Peter nodded with a smile. Everyone was stunned.

"But that didn't show up on your file Peter. I checked you out myself. I brought you under my wing after exhaustive testing. How could I not know? I seem to be working in some sort of a bloody vacuum," complained Mike angrily.

"Even I didn't know until I saw my father's photo in the despatch and then the papers . . . the same face that was shown to me by the solicitor after my mother died. Apparently, he did not know that he had a son. She kept it a secret from him. She was the only one who knew. Her name was Elaine Foster," said Peter, turning to look at the reaction on Mike's face.

"Oh my god . . . no, that can't be. She died in Berlin more than twenty years ago. She was working with me in Eastern Europe. She was my greatest loss . . . all because of her attachment to an East German spy by the name of . . . Sandberg. She died. We retrieved her badly burnt body and buried her outside London. I just can't believe it! After all these years of grieving for the loss of my dearest friend," cried Mike in a panic.

Peter looked at him and smiled.

"No Mike. She wasn't lost at all. Davis secretly helped her to escape to Greece where she hid out for the remainder of her days in the Greek Islands. They never contacted each other ever again for fear of blowing her cover. She had been badly burnt but apparently recovered well. I was born there. She looked after me until I was two years old before sending me to England where I was looked after by her sister as her own. I was only contacted last year by her estate, to set the records straight. She eventually died from complications because of her previous injuries," continued Peter.

"What a complex world we live in. Such protection of loved ones, even in the face of great danger or death," said Robbie quietly.

"Aye, our Mister Davis seems to be larger than life alright," added Harry.

Ruby thought about the last time she had seen Davis. She looked over to a stunned Mike Miller who had obviously suffered the loss of a respected field agent . . . and maybe more. He had been dealt a blow that he would have to deal with later. He took a deep breath and steadied himself for the work ahead.

"What we have here is a strange situation alright. It seems that the past has thrown up some facts that were meant to be buried forever. Now, we must get this Feliks and at least close that part of our situation."

There was no time to dwell on the matter. Mike was devastated but had a quick look at the list. He could see one coded name that he recognised immediately – it was 'Painter Revolver', the code name for Mary Turner. He shook his head and sighed.

Harry got an SMS message on his phone and as he casually looked at the contents, his expression changed to horror. The mood changed instantly.

> "Quick, all of you! Get ready for an imminent attack. The police and intelligence guys on the ground floor have been removed and those from the lift area are dead. My lads say that four men with packages were seen pulling them into the lift. They are coming up here!"

Mike pressed his emergency communicator and shouted for backup.

> "Fourth Floor, four down at ground level . . . Four shooters in lift. Look out for ex-Legionnaires probably carrying weapons. They are with us . . . repeat, they are OK, but take no chances. Shoot to kill anyone suspicious."

Ruby jumped off the bed as Robbie and Harry both removed hidden guns from their inside jackets. Harry had brought two guns . . . he shoved one into Ruby's hand. Ruby pushed it way. She already had the gun that used to belong to Davis in her hand. Harry looked surprised. Carefully they opened the door. Two staff members were walking around heading for the main staff room and there was a trolley bed covered with sheets close to the lift.

> "Get inside your safe room and lock the door," shouted Mike to the staff.

Peter ran to the end of the corridor to secure the stairwell whilst Mike waited outside across from the lift. He looked back at Ruby struggling to come to terms with the latest development.

> "Ruby, you're not well enough yet . . . Go with Harry now and protect them!"

The lift had reached the third floor.

"Harry, Robbie you go with Ruby to Milly's room. Guard her and do not come out until you're told. I'll handle the men in the lift when it arrives. They only have one exit point," continued Mike reaching for his gun and a magazine clip from under his arm.

The ex-Legionnaires were racing up the stairs to get to the fourth floor before the lift arrived. They were exhausted, but punched their way through the pain. Frantically leaping onto the final step onto the fourth floor landing, they rushed at the door . . . it was locked. There was no window.

The fireproof door meant for high security had been activated by Peter from the inside. He waited with gun drawn. It looked like a two-pronged attack to his reasoning . . . the lift and the stair well. The lift reached the fourth floor. The door opened. The four men burst out firing, expecting to a confrontation by a large force.

Mike raised his gun too late and was shot before the lift door had opened. As they started firing their automatic weapons immediately the doors started to open . . . he was already falling to his knees, taking the full force of the ensuing attack. He took the full load of automatic fire from their sub-machine guns.

Suddenly, more shots rang out in rapid succession from across the corridor. They came from two handguns fitted with silencers, fired by an unknown person lying in wait under the sheets on that patient trolley.

'Duff, duff, duff, duff, duff, duff . . .'

The attackers fell one after the other, unable to move to respond in time to the shots, which seemed to have no origin.

Peter remained at the stairwell waiting for more attackers to break through but there was silence. The ex-Legionnaires had managed to smash their way through the security door using the fire emergency axe and it soon became apparent to Peter that the men breaking into the corridor from the stairwell were Harry's men. They were now looking through, into to the corridor. He threw his handgun away into the dead assailants then opened the door to let the tired Legionnaires in, to survey the now quiet but bloody scene . . . with five dead people on the floor covered in blood.

Harry, Robbie and Ruby crept from behind their door cautiously as a lone figure with two guns sat on the trolley, pointing the guns around the corridor as each group emerged. The figure seemed frozen in time . . . but ready to shoot anything that looked unfamiliar.

"Don't shoot my men. They're with me. It's all over. Don't shoot," shouted Harry to the sentinel protector.

Then he looked in disbelief as the familiar figure turned around.

"Tian, Tian, you have saved our lives again. How did you know that these men were coming to get us?" screamed Ruby, as she cautiously went up to greet her.

Tian looked dismayed at what she had done. She had killed four more people. She looked at the body of Mike Miller and shook her head. The others watched on as Tian covered up Miller's body with a sheet.

"The Russians want your list too . . . and were prepared to send in as many people as it takes to get it. This is not the end until we have acted on that list, removing the moles. We have been monitoring this group of mercenaries for some time."

The ex-Legionnaires were plainly relieved and just stood looking at the carnage, realising that their days of adventure were well and truly over. They were out of breath and their bodies ached from the strenuous running up the stair well. The body count could easily have included them . . . and affected their own families.

Harry and Robbie went over to Mike's body where Peter was now standing to check if there was anything that could be done. Mike's body had been torn apart during the attack.

"He was in love with my mother you know . . . and she with him before being betrayed," sighed Peter as Tian took a closer look at him.

Robbie put his hand on Peter's shoulder.

"Looks like your mother was good at keeping things to herself Peter, for the sake of protecting other people's feelings and their lives."

Harry glanced over to his ex-Legionnaire friends and sighed.

"Aye lads well done, but I think we need to stop pretending that we are still good enough to keep doing this. We have our own families to look after lads . . . and here is where we should leave the past. It's gone lads . . . we just get in the way. We are getting too old for this. It's a young man's job," lamented Kippo to his men.

The police and intelligence units arrived within minutes of each other. They all looked ill prepared for what had just happened.

"Aye and where were you all when we needed you? Can you see why we have to look after ourselves?" queried Robbie angrily.

"You'll find Mike Miller over there too . . . he died protecting us. He was a fine man after all . . . aye, but you'll be wanting to know that Tian over there . . . she is the one who single-handedly destroyed the attackers," said Harry proudly.

"We can't rely on you people to look after us. You have a flawed system . . . but unfortunately we still need your help with collecting information," jibed Ruby.

"And just who might you be Miss?" asked the SWAT team captain sarcastically.

"I am Ruby Peters, now an ex-MI6 field operative. I will do anything to hunt down this Feliks monster, to avenge my Eric and then unmask the double agents within your broken organisation . . . because it is plainly obvious that you lot can't do anything anymore," she replied angrily.

Peter was having a few quiet words with his own field operator and turned towards Ruby with a look of apprehension.

Tian gave Ruby a hug, whispering, "We will do this together Ruby . . . for all those who have given their lives for us."

Harry and Robbie shared a quiet moment as they looked on at the four unsettled ex-Legionnaire friends of theirs, still catching their breath. Harry turned back towards Ruby and Tian.

"I'm taking everyone up to Scotland lassie . . . we will all be safe up there . . . whilst you sort this all out. Aye . . . I think you are the only ones able to do it. You'll no have to worry about us at all. It will be a load off your mind. You do your old man proud, Ruby," said Harry firmly, nodding his head.

Ruby nodded with the same simplistic non-emotional acceptance that Harry always used to let her know when she had done well. Harry was so very proud of his daughter. She had repaid her father for all the effort he had put in, in bringing her up to survive against all odds . . . nicknaming her at the age of five, with a name that they only shared together.

"I hope you include me in your team . . . Scarlett," said Peter quietly.

Ruby looked back at her smiling father. Yes. Yes, that was the name he had given her as a child . . . Scarlett!

Tian looked warily at a smiling Peter and then mentally started judging distances and the timing of events leading to the death of Michael Miller. He had been shot moments before the lift door had opened, enough for the attackers to gain the advantage. They had not counted on Tian waiting in her hiding place.

She walked down the corridor away from the group and used her communicator to demand that their forensics team closely examine all the bullets that had struck Michael Miller. She then put in a report to someone much higher up than Henry Roberts.

# Quo Vadis Feliks?

On a small barge resting alongside the banks of the Thames, an agitated young man was becoming delusional and suspicious of his surroundings. His activities during the night had included breaking into a pharmacy for drugs and a small supermarket for food before settling in to his claustrophobic accommodation.

He had been awake for three days and was very edgy but still acutely alert. There was blood on his hands and clothes. Where did it come from he wondered as his mind wrestled with reality. The phone rang. It startled him. He let it ring off before slowly walking over to see if there was any message. After a few seconds, the blue LED started flashing. He wondered who it could be.

He picked up the phone and stared at the brief message line that was still on the screen. Then the screen went blank. He phoned his message bank to retrieve the information that the caller had left.

"Feliks, we need to talk. See you in church at ten thirty."

Feliks was jolted back into real time as he checked the clock to find it was 8-30am. He began to remember the previous night . . . and the things that he may have done. His mind skipped to that slip of a girl who had been waiting on a dark street under the street lamp. She had been hanging around the supermarket laneway soliciting business and had unfortunately caught his eye. She had long hair. That was all.

He was jolted back to the bloodied body parts that were now strewn all around him, all battered and slashed. His quick glance at her face caught the glint of a knife protruding from her left eye.

Cleaning himself up as if nothing had happened and putting on another clean but wrinkled shirt was all he thought about to look more presentable for his meeting. The blood spatters on his trousers would have to stay. He looked at them quizzically, making out familiar faces from their patterns.

Reaching for his jacket, he headed for the stairs up to the deck, taking another sideways glance at the young woman's limp body lying broken and bloodied on the cabin floor.

He remembered that she had laughed at his crazy idea of his being chosen by God to protect her from anyone who tried to make out with her, other than himself.

She would laugh no more. Feliks had smothered the life out of her and cut her to bits with a carving knife in another frenzied attack, before feeling instantly gratified . . . but that was last night.

He had enjoyed the acts of cruelty at the time but now felt hopelessly depressed. He actually felt sad for the way she looked and took a closer look at her blood-matted hair but felt no remorse. He heard voices and saw faces in the windows, and on the water and on inanimate objects. They would not leave him alone.

One was the face of the person who he thought was destined to kill him, searching even now to find him, to hold him down and torture him. Her determined face was indelibly imprinted into his tormented mind. He was on the path to self-destruction. He saw it written in her blood.

People avoided his wild stare as he walked with an unusual gait towards the nearby church. He had been there before.

A wave of anxiety rushed his mind as he imagined Ruby with eyes the colour of blood within his fractious daydreaming, stabbing wildly at his supine body . . . screaming at him, describing all the things he had done to his many victims, starting from when he was just twelve years old.

Meanwhile, a message had arrived to Ruby's phone.

> 'Meet me at St Paul's Church, Winston Heath at eleven. I will have Feliks there in a safe situation. Come alone. We can handle this issue ourselves: Henry Roberts.'

Ruby was at first ecstatic that Feliks had been captured. She showed the message to Tian and later to Peter. Now that Ruby and Eric's family had all been isolated at a secret location in Scotland, guarded by Robbie, Harry and the lads, Ruby felt that the risk of anyone else in her family getting hurt, was now extremely low.

> "I'll go with you as backup Ruby. Don't worry, I'll be very discreet and stay in the shadows outside," offered Peter.

> "I will stay away this time Ruby . . . too many people can make for a very nasty development and may interfere with Feliks' arrest. I don't know why Roberts wants to handle this himself . . . maybe he can't trust his people yet, until the mole is uncovered. Remember to keep Feliks alive for justice to be done Ruby. You are like my sister and I tell you that you will regret harming him. He is a sick man," replied Tian looking at Ruby in

a way that made Ruby aware that there were deeper issues at hand.

"I'm all for justice alright Tian. I'll think about what you said. So, right then, let's head off, it's going to take a while in this traffic," finished Ruby briskly.

Tian was weighing up her next moves to allay her fears about Henry Roberts and now the motives for Peter wanting to be meeting with him and Ruby . . . and the maniacal Feliks.

Feliks had arrived at the church early and was met by one of the priests who happened to see him sitting quietly in a corner, rummaging through the bible. He had torn out a page and was mumbling the words to himself as if it was a sign for him to follow. He heard footsteps.

The priest approached slowly and smiled at him, alerting Feliks with his distorted imaginings to yet another face of the trickery of Satan. Spotting the bloodstains on his trousers and analysing his dishevelled look, with crumpled shirt and tangled hair, the priest began to talk softly, trying to prompt this person to start a conversation.

"I don't want to pry . . . but if there is anything you want to ask from me, or tell me, then we can either talk right here . . . or I can be completely detached and listen to your sins in the confessional over there. No one else will know what you have said, and I can advise you . . . and forgive you for all your sins."

Feliks looked at the priest, smiled softly and pretended to be a vulnerable, troubled young man. One who would be the perfect candidate for being absolved of his evil sins.

"Thank you father . . . yes, I have sinned . . . and I want you to hear everything . . . all the details of my sins . . . and then forgive me. Yes, I think I would like to be heard in the confessional," replied Feliks.

The priest led the way and showed Feliks the entrance to the confessional. There was a prolonged silence.

"You can begin anytime . . . maybe we can start with your name?" said the priest with a sigh, settling into his comfortable routine.

"Feliks is my name. It is derived from the Latin, father. It is supposed to mean happy, lucky . . . or successful."

"I see . . . and are you happy Feliks? Luck and success you know are merely part of a more materialistic lifestyle. Luck and success come from chance, fate or whatever else you may call it. A bit like gambling maybe . . . but being happy . . . well that's what we all want out of life isn't it. So . . . are you happy Feliks?"

Feliks was quiet, but then priest began to hear some sobbing and whimpering.

"Feliks . . . maybe you can tell me about your sins now? Please just take your time."

The priest waited a good ten seconds. He could make out the outline of his subject who had now rested his face against the grill trying to look in. He was breathing deeply.

"Yes . . . oh yes . . . I need to tell someone about my sins . . . for I have really sinned . . . and maybe it is better if I could explain it visually father exactly what makes me so happy," screamed Feliks as he rushed around to the priest, grabbing his throat until not a sound came out.

Not one more gasp for breath was forthcoming. Feliks looked at his watch. He still had another fifteen minutes before Henry Roberts would be showing up for their . . . talk.

After ten minutes, Feliks emerged from the confessional. His crumpled shirt was now soaked in blood. His hands had smeared blood on to his face but he had a radiant smile.

At ten o'clock Roberts entered the church and glanced around cautiously to see where his maniacal 'helper' could be. He never knew what to expect from the often rambling neurotic figure who had the look of neglect and was easily provoked. From behind a curtain near the altar, a familiar voice rang out.

> "Henry . . . stay where you are . . . I am not going to reveal myself to you . . . I look quite terrible today . . . lack of sleep and looking like the rough end of . . . well whatever it is that is very, very rough," said Feliks jokingly.

Roberts was not interested in seeing him at all. He was only there to deliver Ruby there for him to carry out his 'peculiar bonding practices', so that he could have reason to shoot him after the deed was done.

Now at least he already had the names on the list and was all about closing off the loose ends to clear his own history. He was sure that Ruby would listen to reason from such a fine interrogator as Feliks. He was so persuasive if not passionate once he got going.

There was also the matter of Peter Richards who he had also arranged to come along. He was now just another loose end. After shooting Michael at the hospital, he knew that it was only a matter of time before forensics would come up with a match for the bullets that struck him first. What a perfect opportunity to dispose of all three of them with a cover-up that would see him cleared of all the evidence he thought, waiting for his visitor.

Sure enough, at eleven o'clock Ruby entered the church with her gun trained on anything of interest. Peter remained outside.

> "Come on now Ruby. I am your senior officer you know. I mean you do work for us . . . well hopefully you

still do. It's just me and you and a somewhat incapacitated Feliks. I know what you have been through and as part of your initiation training . . . well, we do have to interrogate our prisoners sometimes . . . and I have chosen this one . . . just for you Ruby," said Roberts firmly.

"And when I am through with him?" asked Ruby staring at his smug look.

"When you are through . . . you will leave and I will get into my car. I have provided this case full of money to give to my snout who delivered Feliks into our care. There's nothing more to do my dear. Oh, he'll probably be found by one of the priests and then the police will recognise him as the serial murderer . . . case closed," answered Roberts smugly.

Ruby walked towards the confession box and looked in the confessor's side. Then she looked into the other side and stared down at the mutilated priest. She turned around ready to shoot, pretending that she had seen nothing, but was met with the close-up face of Feliks who was smiling at her like a man possessed with wild eyes and a butcher's knife.

He pushed her slowly into the cubicle as she screamed for help. Her hand holding the gun was trapped against the side of the confessional. Panic set in and she was incapacitated.

"What's going on here?" shouted Peter rushing in, causing Feliks to stop momentarily.

"Help me Peter, it's Feliks and he is going to kill me," screamed Ruby from her muffled mouth.

Roberts looked up lazily at the distraught Peter.

"Oh Peter, glad you could make it lad. Here's the money I promised you for delivering our dear Ruby for her final meeting. Why it could almost be a wedding of sorts. Now then, I've seen that list lad and I believe you are on it. You have been outed by Ruby here who is now indisposed to having her mouth sealed by the kiss of death."

Peter felt sorry for Ruby and struggled not to think of what was happening. He was in too deep. His own life took priority over interfering with Roberts and Feliks and he did not want to underestimate Roberts, who may have included his own demise.

If he could take out Roberts and then Feliks after he had finished his work, then he would be in the clear. Peter swung around to make out that he was concerned, but he was now ready to shoot and kill his careless supervisor.

"You can't harm Ruby by handing her over to that animal. He needs to be put down immediately."

'Duff, duff' – two shots were fired. Peter Richards was dead.

"Then you're no good to me any more Peter . . . but it was fun having you along for the ride," he whispered as Peter sunk to the ground.

Peter had never wanted Ruby harmed but now the search for the list and his indecision to help her sooner had led to his death.

Feliks turned back towards Ruby to continue his work whilst Roberts looked at the case of money, nodding his head and murmuring to himself.

"Davis, you smart-arse bastard. You found out the moles and you got the list delivered . . . but only to me. And it didn't cost me a damn cent."

He could not bear to listen to the scrambling and screaming going on inside the confessional and took the briefcase as he ran outside towards his car. The money was destined for the mercenary group who had helped him clear his muddied name.

Ruby was fighting for her life, fending off Feliks who had already delivered his first strike to her left arm, holding her other arm with the gun. He was now frantically hacking at her long hair in a wild frenzy. It had always reminded him of his mother's hair.

'Duff, duff'

Feliks was dead. Shot from the other side of the confessional. Ruby was crying and in shock as she fell down onto the priest's mutilated body, holding her arm that had been slashed by the knife. She quickly realised that it was not her arm gushing with blood . . . the artery had not been severed but it was Feliks' body slumped over hers . . . it was his blood spurting over her face.

Two hollow-point bullets had pierced his head, severing the carotid artery in his neck and exploding his brain within the cranial tomb of his twisted mind.

As she looked up from her hopelessly trapped position, past the staring eyes of Feliks' destroyed head and feeling his warm blood oozing over her body, a small white hand reached out from what may well have been the heavens.

> "I've come to take you home Ruby. It is all over, I promise you. It is finished."

It was Tian, urgently trying to extract her from the bloody mess. She pulled the terrified Ruby out of the confessional and led her to a nearby seat. Then she called in on her communicator.

> "We're coming out, Ruby and me. There are two down, Richards and Feliks. Roberts is in his car but everything has been taken care of . . . as instructed."

After cleaning Ruby up enough for her to feel a little refreshed, they both went outside to be met with a dark blue Bentley that glided to a smooth stop.

The window wound down slowly. A familiar face stared at her as she was being tended by Tian, with her ruffled matted hair and blood-soaked clothing making for a pitiful sight.

The look on the man's face was like that a parent might have to farewell a dying child. He had a tear in his eye. He got out of the car and gently helped her in, covering her body with his coat, taking no notice of the blood oozing all around him. Ruby had nothing to say. She was spent.

> "You need to rest. Find peace Ruby. It is the way of the Tao that guides you," said Mister Tan softly.

Tian got in the car and looked at Ruby and her father.

> "Thank you father, Ruby will now see the plan that I have for breaking the final link to her troubles, the highest mole that has ever breached the great MI6 and has caused us all so much pain."

Ruby looked at Tian. She always seemed to be there to protect her.

> "Thank you Tian. I can never repay my debt for all the times you have stepped in to save me. I don't know what to say."

> "There is no debt between us Ruby. We are a close family who look after each other," she replied.

The Bentley sped off from the church. Tian had detailed the events to someone 'high up' at MI6, confirming that Feliks and Peter Richards were dead and that Roberts was . . . somewhat caught up in his own plan . . . heading for a misadventure of his own making.

Ruby thanked Mister Tan and Tian once more and watched with interest as Tian brought out the special homing device that Eric had made for her.

> "We believe in natural justice Ruby . . . it is part of our culture. I think Henry Roberts would not like the fact

that your hair-grip is going to bring his downfall," said Tian.

"How do you mean?" asked Ruby.

Tian didn't answer. Ruby looked ahead to see if she could see Roberts' car or any indication as to what was happening. They had been following the car from a safe distance, across the bridge, down onto the freeway and eventually into where they least expected it would go . . . the safe house that everyone seemed to know about, filled with sympathisers from many disgruntled mercenary splinter groups with a patchy allegiance to the Russians.

As Roberts' car pulled up, several men surrounded him to check that he had retrieved the briefcase containing the money.

"Here, press this door-bell to see who is home," said Tian to Ruby, looking straight ahead at the car.

Ruby was unsure what would happen but willingly pressed the button on what looked like a key fob.

'Booooom' The ensuing explosion destroyed Roberts' car and everyone in and around it. The house now extensively damaged was on fire . . . what was left of it.

"No . . . there's nobody home today," said Tian solemnly.

Mister Tan looked at Ruby's surprised face. He nodded to Tian.

"I hope the Russians find all the pieces so that Roberts can be blamed for being a double-double agent. I think you need to get another job Ruby. Your boss has just been fired," he said with a grin.

The Bentley turned around and headed back to London.

"Where are we going now?" asked Ruby.

Mister Tan looked at her carefully then looked straight ahead.

>"I will take you to our own medical facilities. There are people who want to thank you for everything you have done. We are Chinese. We have our own masters. You will be looked after very well . . . and give my regards to Harry, your father . . . and my condolences to Robbie and Milly Johnson. We feel their pain as well and we will honour brave Eric at another time if that pleases you Ruby."

Ruby looked at him and then at Tian who was obviously thinking about Ilya.

>"And Ilya too . . . we must honour him too and remember him," replied Ruby sadly.

Mister Tan nodded, briefly closing his eyes. Tian smiled sadly. Now was the time to grieve her loss of Ilya in her own way.

It was also time for Ruby to finalise her amazing trail of events that had transpired since the day Davis had recruited Eric and herself, in Dogbol . . . when she was just sixteen and when Eric was just that boy at school.

It was a time of innocence.

# Jigsaw

Ruby had been given time off from her work, provided that she underwent a debriefing session and handed over the original list of double-agents which had caused so much trouble and cost many lives.

She took the list out from her handbag and looked at the names, now knowing who the people were. It was important to double-check just in case there had been any mistake. She was confident that Eric had the names right. The actions of the people involved had proved that beyond doubt and they were now all dead. The threat was over. Two words did not seem to refer to diamonds: 'Recall' and 'Switch'.

Maybe they just related to the day when Davis swapped one of the diamonds for another he had engraved with the list. Ruby did indeed 'recall' the day of the 'switch'.

She was picked up by a black Range Rover the day after her break and eventually arrived at the office of Reginald Southern, otherwise known as 'C', the head of MI6, a.k.a. the man with the 'green pen'. It coincided with the designated time for his meeting with the heads of department of MI6, MI5, GCHQ, COBRA and the NCA.

Ruby was quickly introduced to everyone at the table. After a short banter wishing her well with her career and offering their sincere condolences for her Eric, they got on with the business. She was up first so that they could all understand how the list was deciphered and exactly who was on the list, before continuing with other business without her.

She had prepared a poster-size copy of the list of double agents to show the group in order to point out all the words and their meanings. She started by thanking Roger Davis for protecting her and her family, and her Eric for looking after her, for saving her life and . . . that he alone had solved the meanings that Davis had encrypted in his letter and that list etched on the face of a diamond.

She made it clear that sadly, Eric was no longer alive and after pausing to compose herself, she asked everyone to remember another person lost . . . and thanked Ilya Kasparov for saving her soul. That was the day when she realised that she could not kill the 'Cigar Club' members based only on her anger for them killing Roger Davis and for shooting Robbie.

Finally, she acknowledged Tian for being somewhat of a shadow, having saved her life on numerous occasions and therefore deserved special credit. The group seemed to know more about Tian than they let on.

Then she launched into her address, hoping that they would now think more about their field operatives and the jobs they were given . . . always at the ready to serve their country.

> "The original A5 sheet of paper from Davis contains some drawings and some text. The drawing depicts two triangles with a curved line, hinting that they should be joined at the base – thus forming a diamond. The next symbol is the Greek letter Lambda which Eric would

have known instantly as the symbol for wavelength. The code K2R4F8 following it indicates that a Krypton Fluoride laser with wavelength of 248 nanometres had been used to etch the diamond.

The words representing the four 'C's of diamond classification are also on that paper. Once we had determined that the names of the double-agents were etched onto the diamonds, actually only one of them, then even my father could read them and did in fact write them down as the list I have with me today.

The names were written in a code that Davis knew Eric would easily solve, which was why he had left the list to me, courtesy of the barman at the Morpeth Arms . . . now also sadly deceased. Eric would have immediately picked out Mary Turner as one of the moles because of her nickname 'Painter' and another word for her surname which is Turner, written as 'Painter Revolve'.

Applying that same logic, the next name listed was 'Rock Wealthy Glasspike' which would become Peter Richards. Peter is ancient Greek for a rock, wealthy becomes rich, and a glass spike is of course a shard.

'Earth-King 100-Lord' can be broken down as Geo for Earth, Roi is French for king thus giving Geoffrey. Then 100 is a ton, and a lord can be a Don as at a university or the head of a mafia family thus giving Tunsdon.

The final one was harder to crack and the outcome had to be very certain. Ford Peels was to become Henry for Ford and Robert for Peel, as in Robert Peel.

As you all know, Henry Roberts was a senior figure in MI6 and his actions resulted in the death of Ilya Kasparov. With Mary Turner he sought to frame me for that murder and by doing so, leaving me vulnerable for an imminent assassination. He is now deceased as well.

Roger Davis had a son he never knew . . . and unfortunately, this Peter Richards of MI5 had also turned against us . . . and is now also deceased. We know as fact that he killed Michael Miller at the hospital where I was recuperating, before the Russian gunmen poured more bullets into him . . . again thwarted by the elusive Tian who killed them each one as they mounted their attack.

Then there was also the young man, whose mother had been involved in an unsuccessful defection involving Roger Davis. He had developed serious mental problems after witnessing his mother's death . . . and having been tortured himself by the Russians . . . all to do with the passing on of this list. He too is now deceased. He killed my Eric . . . and . . ."

She stopped for a few seconds to compose herself before continuing.

"All these names have now been accounted for in their actions with two being under arrest and two having been killed. Many more people have died trying to obtain this list . . . including my Eric. I doubt that it was worth the loss of so many people but for Eric and me, well we never had a choice in the matter. We were caught up within a never-ending spiral of random attacks against us and our families. Now it seems it was all arranged and coordinated by Henry Roberts who had managed to recruit some allied forces with grievances against our intelligence services."

Ruby looked at the gathering. They were at first quiet then slowly, some smiled, some clapped and others looked horrified.

"Thank you Ruby for your excellent presentation and your kind, heart-felt words you have used to allow us to acknowledge Roger Davis, Eric Johnson, Ilya Kasparov and Tian. I can certainly assure you that the people seated here today know how much you and your family have endured some very dark days. But, I wish you well and a speedy recovery and hope that you continue your service with us in some way, for you will be sadly missed if you leave. We really do need you here Ruby with us. I hope you will consider this once you graduate," said "C" passionately.

The entire meeting erupted into applause and whistling as Ruby was escorted out of the room and down to a waiting car.

She eased back into the leather seat . . . but could not hold back the tears. The specially chosen driver looked at her as like a daughter, deciding that it was best to give her some space and to wait until she had relaxed more.

"You deserve to have some time with your family Ruby. My name is Phillip and I have been directed to take you to your parents in Scotland . . . if that is alright with you?" he said calmly and cheerfully.

Ruby nodded and quietly replied.

"Thank you Phillip, I really miss them. They will be so happy that it is all over."

Ruby had another week off work to see her family to reassure them that all was now safe before her return to London. She was booked in to a safe house on her return, to resume her classmates and assessor to decide the subject for her CCP Practical, the final part of her graduation process.

The CCP project had a most unusual aim and methodology.

# CCP Practical

Ruby's first day back at the office was understandably difficult for all those around her. Pauline Maxwell from HR had advised staff on what to say and what not to say to her. After all, she had lost her long-time boyfriend because of company business and prior to that was all the Roger Davis stuff.

They also knew that she had been setup from within the organisation in which they worked. They had been told that the people who had 'jumped ship' had now been removed from office . . . or were 'dead as a result of resisting capture' as Pauline had put it with a bit of spin.

The rest of Ruby's class had finished their practical assignments and were now working on taking their final oral examination. Ruby was called in to see Pauline.

> "Hello my dear, it's so nice to have you back. Look . . . I know what you have been through and that it has been very tough for you and your family . . . and yet here you are, back in the fold to complete your practicals. Now

then, you are left with just the one practical, the Covert Community Project, or the CCP as it is known. If you did not already know, it's all about staying out of sight, out of mind while you covertly investigate the life of someone that you don't like and they most certainly didn't like you . . . and all without them knowing. You must investigate their lives in order help them out of any problems that they may have, presenting evidence of this benefit within your final report to us. It is your final graduation project."

Ruby screwed up her nose but settled down for what was to come.

"Now then, I believe you used to know a girl at your school . . . a bit of a bully according to your psych testing . . . and part of a gang that harassed you for years . . . by the name of . . ."

"Noooo. Not Blizzard Face?" Ruby whined.

Pauline looked at her with amusement.

"Well if that's the pet name for a Rosemary Winters then yep, that's the girl alright," she replied with a smug smile.

Pauline threw the file over to Ruby who caught it by one edge. Flicking through it with a bored look on her face, Ruby could see that it had basic notes about how to proceed, with milestones to reach along the way. There was a photo of 'the girl'. Some items had to be ticked-off, as when certain information about them had been verified, while others had to have an assessment rating of one to five based on the effectiveness of her actions in solving the person's problems.

"You have one whole week to do your surveillance, ask questions about her, find out what she is doing, what problems there might be and solve them if you can . . . and then to submit yourself and the report for an oral exam by the other students in your class. It's a pity you didn't see any of theirs, but I can tell you that you didn't exactly miss that much. God help us all," rattled Pauline briskly.

Ruby was going to ask a question but wisely held back.

"Right then, on your way girl. Your best bet is to find out more about her family, where and when she was born, what her parents do . . . oh, you know. All those absolute basics first," continued Pauline, heading towards the door in a rush.

Then she was gone. Ruby closed up the folder. Ruby could sense that the other students were watching her. Quickly glancing around, she imagined they had turned away and were pretending to be working.

"You'll be fine Ruby . . . you've had more experience than us. This will be a walk in the park for you," whispered Alan who was nearest the door.

He always seemed to be hanging around her during class and pushing his way into sitting with her or near her. He was becoming a bit of a nuisance that she would have to sort out. Ruby just sighed and sauntered slowly out of the room and along the corridor, much to the delight of the others who could see what was going on with Alan.

When she got back to the safe house, Ruby picked out the first few pages of the project folder and decided that she would have to visit the 'births and deaths' in Doulton.

She now had a new car too, with the last one towed away by MI6 for further analysis. Badly damaged in the accident to start with, it suffered further damage at the hands of the eager forensics team. The old car also brought back bad memories and the 'company' had decided to write it off in the end, compensating her with a nice new Suzuki four-wheel-drive.

There had been an attached whimsical note saying that it was good for 'escaping busy traffic and gridlock'.

Ruby turned on the Satnav to escape the London boundary and headed off to Doulton. At the back of her mind was the urge to see her old house in Dogbol or what was left of it after the explosion. It worried her that she may not cope.

Then there was the Mayfair Mews, the previous home of poor dear Eric . . . and Robbie and Milly. The hotel was up for sale as Robbie and Milly and Ruby's parents Harry and Debra were still in a safe house in Scotland, settling into the peaceful country life within a gated acreage. They loved it there but Milly still missed running the hotel.

Ruby had a plan for that too. Well, it was Ruby and Eric's plan for her four diamonds to be appraised, ready for selling. It was estimated that they were worth up to four hundred thousand pounds, which quite astonished Ruby. It had Eric secretly planning a buying spree for new computers and maybe a boat. There was no thought of that now Eric had gone.

Out of three diamonds, she had decide to give one third of the proceeds to Robbie and Millie to help them find a new place and one third to her own dear parents for just being there for her. The remainder she would use wisely . . . but could not bring herself to buy any property. Not at the stage she was at, with her current emotions and the need to find her niche in the organisation. That was if she intended to stay with MI6.

The final diamond, the one with the engraving of that list of moles would be broken up into smaller diamonds whilst she supervised. As she had worked at the jewellers in Doulton during one summer holiday from school, she decided that Mister Priesner would be the one to destroy the original list forever.

On the approach to Doulton, she waited until last second before finally swerving into the exit road heading to Dogbol.

She just had to see her old village again, if only to calm her mind that she had indeed managed to confront her past demons. The Mayfair Mews was closed. A large 'For Sale' sign was pasted over with 'Sold'. The front entrance from where she was kidnapped was now covered in leaves.

Ruby almost expected to see Eric run out and wave to her just as he did when the school bus used to pull up outside . . . but she had put that thought to rest early on. She knew he would never be coming out of that wine cellar. His funeral and burial wore very hard on her, her friends and colleagues. Eric though had managed to get his own way at his end and have the last laugh, having his own words engraved on the gravestone: 'I'm going to live forever . . . .'

He had joked about it for years, saying that anyone who was at the cemetery sadly visiting the grave of a loved one, just might find a quiet moment to smile back at him.

She had tried to block seeing Eric's final moments from her mind as she continued on down the road until reaching the place just before the sweeping bend, where yellow lines still marked the positions of the shootings that went on there, right outside her house.

White crosses marked the positions of the bodies. On that stretch of the road, there were five crosses – one marking the last stand of Roger Davis and next to that, a similar marked cross for his friend Barrie Barnes. The two unmarked crosses in front of them were the final resting places for two CIA rogue agents.

Around the bend near a tree was the place where one of the Cigar Club members by the name of Cartwright was shot and killed by Tian. He was the evil monster who had murdered the other four by stealth and cowardly assassination.

She looked down at the broken front gate and the charred shell of her burnt, derelict house still surrounded by barrier tape. The house where she had lived for sixteen years had been destroyed as was her desire to stay in Dogbol, or Doulton for that matter. Ruby put her foot down and sped past the exact place where Roger Davis died. This part of her memory was not so easily erased, as was seeing Eric's body, tortured and butchered by a lunatic. Maybe one day, these memories would ease but would not be totally. How could they be?

Ruby chose to drive on the back road towards Doulton. She had phoned up the Births Marriages and Deaths there to make an appointment using a false name, with fake I.D. She hoped that the spontaneous events to follow would ease her painful memories.

Visiting Doulton was one tick off the list of activities – she had gone undercover in the same way that Roger Davis used to do. Pulling over to change her number plates was another tick. Of course she could have rented a car to do her work, but then it was all at her expense and she could now have a better room at the hotel.

"So what name do you think Ruby will use for this last assignment?" Pauline from HR had asked her associates at work who were all eager to follow Ruby's strange working mind.

The options were quite limited with a mind focussed like hers on the job rather than the smaller details of her cover. They all agreed that it would have to be 'Scarlett' as a first name, with the second name probably being a joke on her employer, but they could not come up with anything in particular.

Unknown to Ruby, her classmates were also following her progress by having another classmate go undercover as part of his project . . . watching and reporting on her! She was therefore unaware that it was that nuisance Alan who had been 'chosen' for the undercover assignment – after much manoeuvring and deceit on his part. He just wanted to be near her. Her classmates thought it would be funny to see how it all turned out.

Ruby's car pulled into the Grand Motel reception bay in Doulton. Wearing a navy blue, figure-hugging business dress, she walked confidently up to the reception desk and slapped her I.D. down on the counter.

"Good afternoon, I am . . ." she started.

"Claret . . . Dee Plant?" interrupted the woman, reading her I.D. carefully looking Ruby up and down.

Ruby looked right back at her over her newly acquired spectacles with a look of superiority . . . and surprise.

"Who? . . . Oh yes, that's me alright, Claret de Plant. I have booked a room for four nights and I have a car with me. Do you have me on your books?"

"Dee Plant . . . well yes, here you are, and . . . here is your room key. It's the first on the right about half-way down. Number thirty six," she replied handing over the only key on her desk.

"That's a mighty unusual name if you don't mind me saying."

"De Plant is French . . . it's from my father's side. He's French too," replied Ruby quickly.

"No, I mean the Claret bit . . . just like the drink. I suppose that's French as well then?" she queried with a smile.

"Oh yes, my father is called Merlot and my brother is called . . . Pinot, but then he is quite a dark sort of chap . . . my brother is . . . Yes, we are a winey lot aren't we?" Ruby exuded quickly.

The receptionist looked her up and down again, unsure what to make of this strange situation before giving a half-smile back. Ruby thought at that very moment that she would just love to be a con artist instead of an undercover agent. What a fun time it would be, to be someone else for a week, to forget her own problems for a while. Maybe she should take up acting as an outlet for her curiosity for people and their expressions she thought.

> "Are you here on business or pleasure Claret?" asked the receptionist as Ruby was leaving.

> "That's right, yes I am," replied Ruby picking up her pace.

Ruby drove her car down to her unit and after opening the door, quickly moved her suitcase inside, flinging it on the bed. Inside was her specially prepared surveillance kit – business cards, cameras, bugging devices and night-vision scope.

She was running late for her appointment after visiting Dogbol. Jumping into her car, she fast-tracked it down to the council offices and took the lift up to the second floor. The office door was open and a stern little man whose face looked like an old prune was sitting with crossed arms and a scowl on his face.

> "You're late! It's four o'clock and ten minutes," he barked.

> "That's alright, so am I. Your clock must be running fast. I only have four o'clock and nine minutes," replied Ruby nonchalantly before introducing herself, "I'm Claret de Plant from the Genealogy Society of Great Britain and Jersey."

The man stayed seated, scrunching up his wizened face as Ruby handed him her business card. It was not turning out to be his best day so far.

> "Right then, so what information do you want then . . . Clarrie Deep Plant?" he asked with another scowl looking at her card.

"Well your name will do for a start. I mean, you are the man I spoke to on the phone this morning I presume?"

"David Rowbotham. I'm the keeper of the books and all," he snapped back.

"Well David, I want the information pertaining to the birth of a Rosemary Winters who still lives in Doulton and attended the local high school about three years ago."

He looked at Ruby with a rather startled expression.

"What do you want to know about my Rosie? What's she done now then? I'm not responsible for every silly thing that she gets into . . . or that boyfriend of hers that she's managed to hang on to," shouted the man with an obvious distaste for the delightful antics of 'Blizzard Face'.

Ruby thought quickly.

"But your name is Rowbotham and her name is Winters. Have I missed something somewhere in our little interlude?" she asked sarcastically.

"I'm her step-dad. Her old man left when she started school, he did. I've brung them up decent and proper. I done the right thing," he replied, now descending into his normal 'out of office' way of speaking.

Ruby decided it was time to leave before she caused a scene by giving him a piece of her mind.

"Well I just want to know her date of birth and who her father was for my records. I am here on behalf of her cousins in . . . err, Norway."

"Norway? Norway? That can't be our Rosie. Her dad was a Winters from Blackpool Central, married my missus Beryl from around here, and Rosie was born in . . . well she's nineteen now . . . so you reckon that up yourself," he bellowed, getting up and showing her out of the office. It was more of a shove.

"Thank you David. You have been soooo helpful. I think just how lucky 'Blizzard' . . . I mean Rosemary has been to have had the chance of another father to take care of her," oozed Ruby as she fell out into the corridor.

David slammed the door and could be heard swearing like a trooper at himself and what he had done for his Rosie.

Ruby got to her car and placed a tick in the square pertaining to 'personal records of subject'. Things were going well so far. The next step was to see where Rosie lived and to catch up with some of her few friends to see what everyone else was doing with their lives. The problem was that she might be recognised. After all, she had gone to the local school there only a mere three years ago.

Ruby looked up from her notes and checked out the side mirror. She always had that chill when she could sense something was wrong. It was just a quick look, but the unmistakable profile and movement of the man who had entered the shop behind her was certainly that blasted Alan Barker creep from her class.

"How the hell did he get here?" she thought.

He was quite interesting to look at but she didn't know why at the time. Maybe it was because he looked a bit like . . . like Eric, although Alan was quite a dozy character. Or, maybe it was because he had that same nerdy outlook to situations as opposed to interacting normally within social solutions. Alan had been such a pest lately and he kept interweaving around her at social events like a cat. Now he had followed her to Doulton.

To make sure it was Alan, she got out of her car and walked around the block so that she was behind the shop. Sure enough, Alan was bobbing around, standing out from normality, trying to get a better look at her car and looking for a good photo. He had a brand new red backpack seated too low, bouncing up and down on his bottom as he walked.

Alan had the fright of his life when Ruby crept up beside him and put her arm around his neck and squeezed tightly. Reluctantly she had to let him go as he struggled for air.

"I think that's Claret de Plant's car Alan. What the hell are you doing here, following me like that?"

Alan was sweating and looked to have a high blood pressure. The new camera he was carrying was dangling in plain view by his side. He covered his left shin, waiting for Ruby's inevitable signature kick. Surveillance was not his forte.

"This is my class assignment Ruby. I have to do what you're doing . . . but you are my subject. You have spoilt it now. That means I will fail," he blubbered with a look of despair.

Ruby thought for a moment. She put off kicking him . . . for a while at least. Maybe this 'situation' could be turned around to her advantage.

"No, not really Alan . . . in fact if we team up, we can help each other with our assignments and get perfect grades. You can help me to get the information I need. Look, here's a good shot for your report!"

Ruby posed in front of him, making silly faces, looking suspicious and then funny. Alan thought she had flipped.

"Take your photos Alan. You'll have stacks more for later. We can stage every event so both of us will look like we are just the best undercover agents around."

Alan looked at first upset and embarrassed but soon realised that she had a good point. They could manufacture each other's project data with perfect photos and predictable timing and sequencing, to make then look damn good for the assessor. Alan smiled at her latest funny pose. He did like her . . . a lot.

"Partners?" he gushed.

"Partners in crime," replied Ruby twirling around the bus stop.

"So, where are you staying then Alan? I'm at the Grand Motel on Main Street."

"I'm at the Downtowner Hotel. Not a bad place, but it still feels like I'm on holidays instead of on a covert assignment," he replied sheepishly.

"And so, are you here as Alan then or somebody else? Yes, indeed I think you are. So, Alan it is. Now let's get ourselves organised. Oh, by the way, that name I gave you earlier is my new undercover name . . . Claret De Plant. Here's my flashy business card."

Alan took the card eagerly to see just what nonsense Ruby had included and quickly homed in on her occupation.

"A gynaecologist?"

"Genealogist Alan, a genealogist. I look up everyone's privates," she replied with a grin.

"Right, a genealogist and I suppose that name is totally made-up, or is it someone from a novel or a film?" he asked slowly.

Ruby looked at him as if he hadn't learnt anything about surveillance, coding or undercover work.

"What colour is claret Alan?"

"Red"

"What colour is a ruby Alan?"

"Oh right, that's red too. Now let's see . . . very smart. De Plant is in fact, the plant, or like a . . ."

"Like an undercover person, planted in a normal social environment," interrupted Ruby, nodding her head, "So let's go back to my room so we can plan out what we are going to do."

Without having the time to answer, Ruby got hold of his tie and pulled him towards her car. She opened the passenger side door and started to push Alan in, brushing his ruffled hair with her hand. Alan thought that Ruby was coming on to him.

"Nice touch with the jacket and tie too Alan especially in Doulton. Good, you can be the researcher from the Government Statistical and Numerological Offices . . . the SNO . . . and you can conduct a snow job Alan, on our unsuspecting interviewees."

Alan laughed along with Ruby but was thinking that if anyone was likely to be covered in snow, it was already apparent that it would be him, for going along with such a ridiculous prank. However, Alan had other things to consider which prompted him to volunteer to do this particular class assignment. There was more to Alan than just being a hapless student with an apparent crush on her.

It took about an hour to work out that Ruby needed some more information about 'Blizzard Face's' parents, relatives and employment details. After working out that several agencies and close friends would need to be contacted, Ruby decided that it would be better to just get the information straight from 'Blizzard Face' herself, now that she had Alan in tow to do the interviewing for her.

First, Ruby agreed to pose for more photographs; at the motel, in her car and at various locations around Doulton, so that Alan could compose a brilliant surveillance portfolio for his project as well as her own. Of course she would have to be suitably dressed and in the right pose to look good in said photos. Alan was in for a right treat. Ruby was very expressive, almost too good for what should have been 'normal' everyday photos, albeit of a spy.

"Here's a good one Alan, this will be perfect for the motel shoot," shouted Ruby cupping one hand to her forehead, staring into the distance.

Ruby then shoved her head out of the motel room door, arm outstretched, head held high with a pout and raised eyebrows. Alan snapped away regardless. He could look at the photos later and ogle over her sensuous body.

Next followed the 'getting in the car'; 'getting out of the car'; 'entering offices'; and 'talking with complete strangers' shots. These strangers such as the other guests and random people that she met in businesses around town were put on record with fictitious names, as official undercover contacts.

Ruby's job was nearly done. Alan's job was half-done. He now had to find a way of interviewing 'Blizzard Face' to get all the required information, without raising concerns or getting himself arrested for misrepresentation.

They both went back to Ruby's hotel room where Ruby went to the bathroom before making them both a coffee. She turned around to find Alan resting on her bed, posed suggestively with a beer in hand from the bar fridge. She felt rather annoyed but the prospect of ending her project early made her easily swayed against her better judgement.

"Don't get too cosy mister or I'll have to shoot you," she joked.

Alan sighed and slowly made his way over to the door with the intention of leaving. Ruby meanwhile had just thought of the perfect disguise for Alan's phone call to Rosie.

However, Alan still wanted to leave, as he was sure that Ruby was making subtle hints for him to go. After more arguing and threatening to walk away from the entire deal, Ruby pretended to offer an incentive.

"Of course, you scratch my back and I'll . . . probably not shoot you . . . Alan," she joked seductively.

Alan was unsure whether she was joking or not but made the phone call to snare the interview. He could be in luck . . . perhaps this evening. He was hooked and tested out his interview voice before making the call.

"Hello. This is Rosie," answered a rather soft voice.

"Well hello Rosie. I am looking for a Rosemary Winters. Is that you by any chance, my name is . . . er, Peter Redford?" asked the politely sounding but unsure Alan.

"Yes, it is. I am Rosemary, but people just call me Rosie now that I've left school you know. What do you want . . . Peter?" she replied, sounding interested.

"Peter Redford," he repeated, "Yes, well I'm from the Government Statistical and Numerological Offices and I'm doing some research on several aspects of what the ex-students of Doulton High School are doing, three years after leaving. You are one of twenty students specially chosen for this project. I hope you have some time to talk with me."

There was a bit of scuffling and the sound of babies crying in the background before Rosie could reply.

"I'm sorry about the noise. Now then, I can only give you a few minutes because my baby needs feeding. So what do you want to know?"

Ruby was listening in and mouthing to herself, "A baby!"

"Thank you for your time Rosie. I would first like to confirm just a few facts that I already have. And, your father's surname is . . ."

He waited.

"King, you should have King, Robert King," answered Rosie.

"Yes, yes I have that. And err you are now nineteen and . . . you have a baby as well Rosie?"

There was more noise in the background.

"Two Peter. I have two children . . . one girl and a boy. David is the baby and there's little Ruby whose three soon," she replied.

Ruby's face portrayed her total shock.

"Ask her where the names came from . . . the babies," whispered Ruby anxiously to Alan.

Ruby moved closer to Alan to listen in. He could feel her warm cheeks close to him.

"Two children. How nice Rosie. Now tell me . . . were your babies named after your mother's side or your husband's or partner's side . . . because of course, you are not necessarily married?"

Rosie took a while to answer.

"My boyfriend will probably . . . well he may . . . we may get married very soon now . . . but it's really not that important to me. My son David is named after David Bowie. He was someone that I looked up to as such a unique individual. And my daughter is named after a friend . . . well not exactly a friend . . . but someone I knew . . . she was really independent and . . . and I thought that I would have liked to have been good friends with her, if things had been different."

"Why? Why?" mouthed Ruby to Alan.

"And why was that Rosie . . . were they just nice people or . . .?"

"Because they were their own people . . . and I was not," replied Rosie, "Well, not until now."

"Well, I suppose you are not in employment then, what with two children to look after Rosie?"

"Oh no! I do work full-time. I did a course in child-care and now have a children's play school at my house. That's why it's so noisy. There are six here today. I can combine being a mum with looking after some other children."

Ruby was beginning to rethink her opinion of 'Blizzard Face' and had underestimated just how much influence the other girls had on her at school. Alan gave Ruby a dirty look and shook his head despairingly.

Alan was certainly warming to Rosie. He looked at Ruby who was giving him the signal to terminate the interview, but then she signalled to ignore it. He just loved her antics.

"Ask her what she would like most," asked Ruby to Alan.

"So, well thank you for talking with me today Rosie. Just one more question if you don't mind. Tell me . . . what would you like the most . . . you know, to happen to you or to be given something maybe, just for the record, to see if you could improve or extend your current expectations and plans?" he asked temptingly.

"I don't even have to think about that Peter. I would want to eventually get married, expand my play school and . . . and maybe find out what happened to the girl whose house was destroyed in Dogbol . . . they say that she has had some very hard times and I want to know if I could help," said Rosie softly.

"Thank you Rosie. I'm sure that you will get everything that you want and especially that your children will be forever grateful for having such a great mother like you," replied Alan quietly.

Ruby was tearing up. How could this be, this bogus event bringing up such information about Rosie and about her own thoughts of the past? It was almost as if everything had been planned to turn out like this . . . to show her more about her inner-self and values. It was topsy-turvy alright.

"She doesn't seem to deserve the nickname 'Blizzard Face', Ruby. I think maybe you have read her wrong. You know, schoolyard play is not like real life. Rosie sounds to me like a really caring person. Well, you've got your information. I'm done," said Alan, sidling up against her and holding her rather closely.

She could feel his breath on her neck and the closeness of his face to her hair, enough to feel a little uncomfortable but not offended. He had downed two beers after all and was just becoming a little more confident, she thought. Then he reached up her back to stroke her neck.

"Well, you don't seem to be reaching for your gun Ruby."

Ruby moved away slowly and managed a smile before confronting him in a way he would understand.

"No Alan. I'm not done grieving for my Eric. I just can't. I'm sorry. You know what happened to him only a short time ago."

Her mind was ticking over with thoughts about Eric and Rosie . . . and about Alan. She thought more about Eric and imagined that it was just the feelings of missing his closeness that had aroused her curiosity to think much further about any dalliance with a pest like Alan. She was amazed that it took a creep like Alan to make her think more about her deeper longing for closeness and to be loved.

"I . . . I just need a few covert photos of Rosie, which I can do by myself and then we can call it a day Alan. I want to thank you for talking with her. I would never have got that information if it had been me talking with her. And I want to thank you for sharing some time with me. It has been very difficult for me to continue working after my Eric's sudden death."

Alan smiled back at her rather smugly as Ruby stared into the distance in a daydream. He left the motel room quickly, heading off to finalise his own project report. She hadn't noticed that he was walking away without his backpack – another oversight. He had hidden it underneath her bed. Maybe he was expecting her to call him back . . . later on, if she changed her mind.

Ruby focussed back on to the job that she was sent to do. Now all she really wanted to do was make amends with 'Blizzard Face'. Her assignment made it clear that she was not to contact her subject directly, so after doing something to help Rosie as stipulated in the project aims, Ruby would have to wait for another time to talk with Rosie face-to-face, maybe over drinks.

That night, Ruby started her report, inserting the photos that Alan had sent to her by email. Some did look a bit contrived, but a bit of editing soon put them in perspective.

The next morning she was up bright and early, heading off to take some more photos of Rosemary Winters, a.k.a. Rosie, a.k.a. Blizzard Face, a mother of two and obviously a much misaligned young woman.

"Hello Ruby. I thought I'd tag along with you, if you don't mind before I have to catch my bus back to London this afternoon."

It was Alan again. He had obviously been thinking that if he was persistent, she may let down her guard. He was smiling and offered her his hand.

Ruby automatically reached for his hand, not knowing why except that it was offered and she didn't know what else to do.

Alan used both hands to greet her and kept hold for a few long seconds before letting go.

They looked at each other briefly before Ruby averted her gaze and started talking about the day ahead. She assumed that this was a clear signal to him that she did not want his attention.

> "Rosie usually goes to the corner shop first thing to buy milk as we know, so that's where my first shot of the day will be. And she'll have her children with her which is a bonus."

> "Any idea what you want to do for her yet Ruby?" asked Alan briskly.

> "Not decided yet. Does that have any bearing on your own report deadline Alan?"

> "Only in that I have to know what you intend to do, what you actually do and to verify that Rosie has benefitted from your actions. But I can do that at another time because it will probably take a while for your actions to take effect. That's why I'm out of here this afternoon. Deadlines are important . . . but they generally take care of themselves with proper planning."

They both waited across the road from the shop. Almost to the minute, Rosie with her children David and Ruby came around the corner. The children were both in the pram. Rosie looked so smart and proud. She had grown up too in those three years.

> "Got them. Time to move on in case she sees me," said Ruby quietly, hoping to ditch Alan sooner rather than later.

> "They look so nice together don't they? To be safe in a family that cares is very important . . . and for them to feel safe . . . is priceless. You never know how your life can change in an instant Ruby, especially in our line of

work," replied Alan sarcastically, staring at her lack of interest in him.

"Yes, I have had some very worrying moments about my family and Eric's. They have been targeted on more than one occasion but at least they are safe now."

"Are they are in one of our safe-houses Ruby?" asked Alan suddenly.

Ruby felt as though her guard had been let down yet again for here was another intrusion into her private space, although in itself the question was quite innocent.

"They are in a private safe-house . . . it is better that no-one knows where they are . . . what with all these double-agents and everything," replied Ruby, looking for Alan's reaction.

"I've heard that your dad and his mates were in the foreign legion . . . wow, that's amazing Ruby. More exciting than what we're doing I think. They would definitely make for a good safe-house, what with their reputation. Your dad's Scottish isn't he?"

Ruby was getting bad vibes about his line of questioning.

"You can't believe everything you hear Alan . . . and what about your family? Aren't they from Poland or some other Slavic country? Barker . . . that isn't Polish though is it, unless it has been changed?"

Alan looked at her with a different attitude. His aim to have a chance at being with Ruby to satisfy his crush had been to no avail. He now only had to carry out his more important orders from outside the 'company'.

"You can't believe everything you hear Ruby," he replied tersely with a faint smile.

His eyes gave away more information for Ruby to assess.

"I'll take some more photos of my other contacts that I have spoken to, and looked up from our databases . . . so . . . I would like to do that on my own if you don't mind Alan. I just need to feel as though I am a free agent and . . . well, you wouldn't be following me around if this was a real covert surveillance assignment . . . would you?"

"Fair enough, no offense taken. I'll be packing up and heading back to London. It's been great fun tagging around with you Ruby . . . I think that we could have made a great team. Take care of yourself. If I can't look after you . . . then . . . well I know how independent you are," replied Alan sharply.

Ruby did not look at him again as she turned and walked in the opposite direction. She now hated him and wondered why he was chosen for the one assignment where he was at licence to get to know her.

Alan's smile tuned into a scowl before he resumed his detached attitude, whistling as he walked down the street.

# Another Tail

Ruby was feeling very happy now that she had revisited her home town. Her views on 'Blizzard Face' had changed. She wondered just what else she had read wrongly during her period of growing up.

Even Eric had been a surprise development at the age of sixteen after originally thinking that she hated him . . . but then at that time she hated everyone and everything for she was so confused about her sense of self. She had finished growing up at sixteen and was now just getting older and hopefully a lot wiser. With her CC Project now complete with background information, photos and current status of her subject, the only thing left to do was to provide some sort of plan to improve Rosie's life.

According to the project rules this was to be done without Rosie knowing, the final phase being a follow-up on the developments to record the predictably planned positive outcome. Her ideas would have to be achievable.

This selfless help to Rosie would have to be something really special and highly beneficial. Apart from a genuine desire to help Rosie, Ruby knew that Alan was doing a similar project based on how she was conducting herself but there was something strange about Alan that she did not like. It was almost as if he was trying to muscle in on her assignment. She also knew that both projects would be debated by their classmates . . . and assessors.

Would he ruin her project because of her rejection to his advances? A crush can sometimes turn into a bitter hatred.

She decided that Alan was to be avoided in all future dealings with MI6 prompting her to take more photos to replace the ones that Alan had taken. It was now three o'clock and she needed to go back to her hotel room to think out her plan to help Rosie.

As she walked along the High Street taking a peak at some of the shop fronts displaying clothes and then looking closely through the jeweller's window at some beautiful wedding rings, she sensed again that someone was following her.

The reflection in the window hinted at some movement across the road from her, moving and stopping almost in sync with her. Ruby had developed her own plan for dealing with such situations. The next shop was the bakery.

Ruby walked in and stood at the counter slightly askew so that her left side exposed the lapel camera to the street. She bought a sausage roll and a coffee and sat down near the window looking out of the corner of her eye.

Knowing roughly where her tail was waiting, she kept the lapel camera trained on the doorway across the road taking a few shots over a five minute period. Then she walked up to the counter behind other customers and took off her coat, turning it inside out. It was now dark blue instead of grey. She pulled up her hair and put on a beret.

As other customers left the shop, she exited with them on the inside, away from the curb. Further up the road, she crossed over and waited in one of the shop doorways, camera again pointing towards the doorway where she imagined the tail to be hiding. Sure enough, there was a man of about thirty years of age judging from his stance, staring at the bakery, slightly agitated . . . hesitant about maintaining his position. He was wearing a hoodie jacket, jeans and off-white gym shoes.

'Snap, snap, snap, snap, snap'

The camera burst captured various angles of the man's face. Ruby spoke into her camera, directing the images for inspection and analysis. The earpiece sprung to life within a minute.

> "Keep your distance! Do not approach the subject. He is armed and dangerous. It is Alan Barker. He has now been analysed and linked to Peter Richards and Feliks Bielski and he may be on drugs. We advise that he is targeting you personally Ruby. Get out of your hotel immediately and wait for backup."

Ruby was instantly aroused and angry as her adrenalin kicked in. She had caught up with the last remnants of the double-agent consortium that had infiltrated MI6 . . . and had murdered her Eric. He had also been with her for over a day . . . touching her, mauling her . . . gaining her confidence and asking questions. She had been right . . . but it had taken too long to make that assessment.

Immediately she raced down the road intent on confronting Alan, fumbling to retrieve the gun that her dad had given her, poised to strike and shoot this man to death. Turning into the doorway with the gun primed for attack, the intensity subsided; Alan had gone; the door was locked with a padlock. He had escaped . . . for now.

She started to backtrack on how Alan could have known where she was at that moment as she had concealed her whereabouts at each step of her travels. Then she realised that as he had volunteered for the class project, he would certainly knew of her position at any time by using his service tagger.

Ruby checked in to base with her updates advising she was leaving the motel and would be heading towards the highway. It seems that Alan's intention had always been to get close to her and her family. He wanted the information for others to 'follow up'. The memory of Alan's questions about Scotland and the Legionnaires rushed her mind. She thought of her family staying up there in their private safe-house. He had not managed to get anything out of her regarding its location.

Ethics and justice had gone out of the window for Ruby as she realised that Alan needed to be eliminated to prevent him going after her family. Even her father would eventually see the logic and necessity to do that without remorse.

She had always wanted her covert surveillance to be of her own time, place and subject, but Ruby now had an assignment within an assignment . . . and she knew which one had priority.

Alan would no longer be able to remain at MI6 anyway because his cover had been blown, so he would be looking to complete his extra-curricular assignment in any way possible.

Ruby ran down the streets leading up to her motel. She had to get out of there immediately and find her way back to the highway, leaving Doulton to wait for backup. As she approached reception, the house cleaner was just opening her motel room door with her trolley standing outside the window.

'Booooooom'

The room exploded, throwing the house cleaner into the car park and sending debris into the rest of the hotel. Black smoke was billowing from where her room used to be.

Adjacent units were on fire. The fire bell was ringing. Then everything was quiet.

Ruby was devastated. She looked all around her for other victims of the bombing . . . and then she caught a glimpse of a grey sedan driving off from the other end of the hotel. The driver was a man in a hoodie. He looked at her briefly. His plan had failed. The driver was unmistakably Alan.

Ruby looked down at the house cleaner's mutilated body smouldering on the ground, now with hotel staff rushing to realise that she had died. They were crying and in shock. Then there was a tremendous smashing sound coming from where Alan's car had disappeared around the corner. It was like the crumpling of metal and the continuing shattering of glass.

Ruby made a call on her lapel phone/camera.

"Ruby to emergency. Bomb explosion at Grand Motel in Doulton. Target was me. Perpetrator was Alan Barker seen leaving the hotel in grey hoodie driving a grey sedan. One woman down at hotel. Another explosion further down the road. Will investigate."

"Roger that Ruby. Keep in touch. Backup is already at accident scene. You are completely safe."

As Ruby rounded the corner the full impact of seeing two cars smashed together with one on fire made her stop abruptly to assess her options. Alan's bloodied body was lying on the road to one side. The windscreen of the car he had been driving had smashed outwards, indicating that he had not been wearing a seat belt.

The other car was a Toyota Land-Cruiser with a massive bull-bar and what seemed like very little damage. The driver was facing away from her but looked like a sports woman wearing a tracksuit and a baseball cap. Ruby deduced that the woman was probably on her way back to the hotel after visiting a gym when Alan's car sped around the corner and crashed head-on into her. However, it was the Land-Cruiser that was now on the wrong side of the road.

Ruby walked over to examine Alan's lifeless body. He had a broken neck and his face was a mess. There was no pulse. Dark black blood was oozing from his open chest cavity. It was obvious that he was beyond repair. She looked up. The woman was standing beside her.

"He is the last one Ruby. That's official. There are no more!"

It was Tian. She was not smiling . . . just looking at Ruby with that protective sister look. Ruby was speechless.

"Tian to control. Alan Barker down. I'm with Ruby. Will investigate hotel bombing and secure area for forensics. All clear at this end," said Tian confidently into her lapel phone.

"How did you know about all this Tian? How long have you been here in Doulton?" asked Ruby, partly in shock.

"I've been tailing you for about the last three weeks Ruby Peters. There are many things you need to learn if you want to stay in the service of MI6 . . . and be able to stay alive in any future operation," scolded Tian.

Ruby was unsure what to think about the outcome of this drawn-out battle with infiltrators and demons from the past.

"But you are not hurt at all. Not a scratch on you . . . but the damage to that car and to Alan," queried Ruby.

Tian managed a slight smile.

"You think I call myself Taipan from the many rumours that circulate around about me Ruby . . . but my codename, should I ever need one . . . would have been 'Teflon'. Not a hard immovable object like a diamond or a ruby . . . but merely a smooth surface with no form, by which to escape and move freely so that I can fight another day. Oh yes, by the way I am of course MI6 as you must have guessed by now. I used to work with Roger Davis on the more delicate assignments, and reporting directly to 'C'."

Ruby just shook her head in amazement.

"You, are working for MI6? You worked with Roger Davis? Why did you never tell me? And how do you explain this well-timed accident and how you came to be exactly in this place . . . at this particular time then?" asked Ruby angrily.

"Oh this is no accident. I planted a homing device on his car and realising he was at the motel where you are staying, I hired this big vehicle to stop him in his tracks. You know, I too failed to see him plant that bomb in your room. I followed you both all day today and I think he only returned to the hotel to see the bomb go off . . . after planting it there when he came to your room yesterday," replied Tian looking disappointed with herself.

"Oh my god, he could have exploded it during the night. All he wanted from me was to verify that the location of the safe-house is in Scotland. It was only that he wanted me to be with him as a token of his exploits that I've survived the night. I've done it again. I've invited people into my space without thinking that they may be out to get me.

The last time I did that was when that lost girl talked to me at the stream near my home and I invited her in to make a phone call for her to get picked up . . . and she turned out to be the one who mapped out my house for a break-in to steal the diamonds. I don't think I'm cut out for this work Tian. I make too many errors."

Tian looked at her closely.

"I will train you myself from now on. There is no going back now. You know too much for one thing and you could never settle down to an ordinary life if you tried. You have the makings for a really good agent because you care but remember that you are representing your country . . . keeping people safe from what could be very nasty consequences of not being prepared," said Tian calmly.

Ruby looked devastated. She had lost friends and had violated her family's safety and she had lost dear Eric.

"You must go and see your family and Eric's family to tell them in person that it is all over. Spend some more time together. Finish your assignment with that Rosie girl . . . she too has had a hard life and could do with something good happening, completely 'out of the blue' as they say."

"Yes. I should be thankful that I have lived through all this. My responsibility is to look after others from now on, to prevent anyone from experiencing what I have seen can happen to everyday innocent people," replied Ruby.

"Come on, let's get this motel business sorted out and pause for a moment to think about that poor maid's family before moving on . . . for that is the first thing you should learn . . . to do what you can for those who are affected by disaster and then move on. This is what your current training is all about . . . an act of random kindness, caring and thoughtfulness for someone you once hated, before resuming your often thankless work," said Tian.

Ruby could not hold back the tears anymore. Tian brought her close and gave her a long hug.

"We're only human Ruby . . . now is the right time to grieve for Eric and Ilya. They will always be with us. Always remember the good times whenever you feel down and hopelessly lost. They will take care of your inner self where you really reside. Everything else is merely external. You only have to imagine that they are there . . . always holding you close," she sobbed quietly.

They shed their tears freely together, oblivious to the gathered crowd surrounding the accident scene. Ruby looked at Tian with a wicked grin.

"You don't want me to die Tian. That's your problem."

# Blue Sky

Ruby slept for a good ten hours back at the safe house. Many years of pain and guilt forced to the surface over the last few weeks were at an end . . . dominated by yet another two deaths. Ruby called her dad in Scotland to say that she would be visiting them in a few days. She had completed her assignment.

Old Harry had few words to say to his daughter as usual but Ruby could imagine him nodding approval at her courage and focussed determination to see things through. He had taught her well. Ruby took a deep breath and started gathering some ideas on how to help everyone and to reward all those who had suffered her pain and their own loss.

She took out an A3 notepad and a new pen. The word 'Rosie' appeared at the top of the page. She circled it, stared at it and thought about how Rosie had named baby David and 'little Ruby'. Looking through Rosie's notes, she picked out her boyfriend's particulars; Lawrence Oates, age twenty, occupation as . . . computer programmer and analyst.

"My god, he went to the same school and . . . why he must have known my Eric . . . yes he has almost the same profile," whispered a surprised Ruby.

There was a phone number and a photograph. He looked familiar but then the I.T. people all pretty much looked the same in official photos. Maybe it was their resentment to the invasion of their personal space that showed up more in photos. Eric was like that at first before he got to know Ruby.

An interesting note scrawled on the bottom of the page showed that Larry's mother had died in a car crash and his father Tony had remarried and had more children. The two did not get on. Now there was another sticking point to overcome.

Putting down Lawrence's profile, she picked up her main subject notes – Rosie Winters. Ruby had found out quite a lot about Rosie - almost too much to bear reading in one sitting. What agony she must have gone through at school being thrust into the role of gang member when her personal life was so dysfunctional and physically painful.

Her mother Beryl was once an alcoholic who had graduated to heavy drinking by way of smoking weed to ease her own problems. After admittance to hospital on several occasions for extensive bruising and fractured limbs, an AVO was taken out on her first husband twice in one year.

Robert King had apparently left home when Rosie was only six. However he had 'left them' for the bleak constraints of Her Majesties care and pleasure. With twenty years to spend in prison for a murder that he said was in self-defence, it was thought much better to just say he'd left home, to protect little Rosie.

Ruby reckoned that he would be out in six more years. This was something to remember for a future day. Beryl even changed Rosie's surname to Winters, convincing Rosie that her real father was killed in a car accident.

Rosie's new Dad of thirteen years, David Rowbotham who used to be an acquaintance of Robert King, had started off not much better, although he was working and provided the family with a place to stay, if not a real 'home'. He had muzzled his way into Beryl's life by supplying her with booze and using the home as a safe place to store stolen cigarettes and liquor.

The only thing for which he could be given great credit was to ensure that the sleazy criminal characters that once came and went from the house at all hours did not touch Rosie.

He had seemingly undergone a remarkable change when Rosie's babies had been born. Maybe he was redeemable. The household had really settled down substantially ever since Rosie started going with Lawrence who was staying with them and paying rent. Then there were the children that Rosie looked after including her own.

These changes to the old routine ensured that David Rowbotham now had more income, on account of Lawrence's rent money and Rosie's childcare cash. Also, Beryl had given up drinking altogether when Rosie's babies had been born and was now more appreciated for having contributed to everyone's comfort with her cooked meals, clean house . . . and sobriety.

David resented Lawrence's intrusion into his house at first but they got along because he knew that David and Rosie could afford to move, taking their income with them, leaving him alone with the new Beryl. Her hands-on response to any of his violent intentions was now an expected painful outcome.

"Hello. Is that Lawrence Oates?" asked Ruby politely.

"Yeah, that's me. That's Larry anyway. Who are you?" he asked rather sharply.

Ruby was already regretting her spontaneous desire to phone him and he did seem rather abrupt.

"I used to go to your school and was going with Eric Johnson. Did you know him at all?"

There was silence at the other end. Ruby waited.

"Yeah, yeah, I knew Eric back then. How's he doing? He was real smart was Eric. So . . . you must be Ruby! I should know that because our daughter is called Ruby . . . apparently after you and your crazy antics," he replied, perking up a bit.

"You're right Larry. I'm crazy Ruby, yes. I wanted to call you because I'm working on a project at the moment and it has to do with your Rosie . . . but I'm not allowed to contact her. I know it sounds strange and everything, but I was hoping you'd help me. It won't take up much of your time . . . I just need some information that's all, before I decide what to do."

"Yeah right, it sounds a bit weird but what do you want to know? I mean how does that affect Rosie? I don't want her getting into any trouble or anything . . . not just before we get married like," he answered all bright and bubbly.

"Married? Wow. Congratulations Larry . . ."

Larry butted in quickly.

"Wait, wait . . . she doesn't know yet. I haven't asked her. I mean I haven't got the ring yet. It's going to be a surprise . . . this weekend in fact . . . when I take her out to dinner."

"Wow, she will be really happy Larry. I think she is looking forward to you proposing to her too," gushed Ruby.

"But how do you know that . . . if you haven't spoken with her?"

"I haven't . . . but I have spoken to a friend of hers that I met recently. I can't think of her name at the moment

. . . but I do know that Rosie will be over the moon if you ask her."

There was a slight pause.

"Wow, that's a relief. So, how can I help you, now that you've given me more confidence to pull this thing off? Just name it Ruby . . . oh, and what is Eric up to these days? Are you still going out with him?"

Ruby was a little stunned but carried on quickly.

"Yes, he is always with me Larry. Always there for me."

"Hey, didn't you used to kick him in the leg all the time?"

"No . . . no, not all the time, only when he told a bad joke . . . Now then Larry, getting back to Rosie. I think that I've worked out what I can do for Rosie already. All I need to know is when you have popped the question and her thoughts on when the wedding will be," said Ruby.

"Oh, now there's a sticking point Ruby. We don't have much money . . . and after querying her previously, she said that she wanted a registry office wedding, on account that we are not religious and only have a small number of friends and family," he said sadly.

"Now that's where I can help Larry. This project that I have to complete is based on helping someone without them knowing and it comes with my company paying for something like a registry office wedding for instance . . . you with me? I mean this is your lucky day," replied Ruby enthusiastically.

"But why did you pick my Rosie?" he asked quizzically.

"Ah, now then, this is a little bit tricky Larry. The person that was chosen for me by my company had to be someone that I hated in the past . . . err, we both hated each other you know at the time, or thought we did anyway. But now you can see that she has named a baby after me, which is absolutely mind-blowing . . . and here am I, able to give her the spoils from my project and later get to know her better . . . if she wanted."

"Do you realise how stupid that sounds and totally unbelievable?"

"Absolutely true Larry. You can ask her yourself, as long as you don't tell her that I spoke with you. Ask her about how she named her little Ruby . . . and I think you'll be surprised alright," replied Ruby.

"Anyway, what do you get out of all this? I mean, how does this thing work and why is it being offered? There must be some catch that I've missed. What's the cost?" he said slowly.

"Right, this it Larry, my company put me on an internship. I have spent the last year working through a tough training schedule and I'm up to my final assessment . . . to do something to help someone that I used to hate, without them knowing . . . and to prove the results in a final report. Apparently it is a test of my ability to act against my nature and show caring . . . oh you know all the fluffy stuff that movies are made from . . . but to be totally distant from any recognition by that person during the process. Now strangely enough, it seems as though my dislike for Rosie and her dislike for me was all bluff and based on poor judgement," said Ruby.

"Wow that is some tough company you work for. It sounds a lot like my team building weekends that we have to go on twice a year. So . . . can you tell me who you work for?" he asked slyly.

Ruby thought about it carefully.

"Well actually it's a company that saves people's lives . . . but I can't tell you the name Larry. I could have lied to you but I think that it's fair to say they are well known . . . but prefer their privacy."

"I think I'll leave that one well alone and not tempt fate by stuffing up a golden opportunity. You would probably have to shoot me if I persisted . . . right?" replied Larry with a laugh.

Ruby gave Larry an ordinary phone number that she had pre-paid just for this project.

"Just text me with a 'Yes' and a rough date and then I'll let you know your options for a fully paid wedding. Rosie doesn't ever need to know the financial details and I'll get the registry office to keep me in the loop with what Rosie is planning. Is that OK?"

"Sure Ruby . . . and thank you for what you're doing. I'm going to ask Rosie about little Ruby's name as soon as I'm home. Give my regards to Eric too. He's one lucky dude. Goodbye."

"Goodbye Larry . . . nice talking with you," she replied softly.

Ruby thought about Eric playing around at school and the time she planted a whopping great kiss on his lips in front of Rosie and her girl gang. Their reaction to that was better than any other confrontations and 'staring out' sessions that she had with them all the time.

She had set her plans in motion for Rosie, Larry and their children David and Ruby. All she needed now was the go ahead and prospective date for the wedding.

Her attention now turned towards her family and that of Eric's. Another idea sprung to mind immediately. Then there was the matter of giving dear Tian something in recognition of her many successful sorties to rescue her and Eric . . . and to show respect for the loss of Ilya Kasparov, her soul-mate.

The knowledge that Davis and Tian had been working together at MI6 at the highest level was more proof that she needed to learn more, faster, better and from the inside. She had no idea. There was much to do. A visit to the bank was her first priority.

Completing the assignment check sheet now only required the verified reaction to her goodwill deed and then an oral examination in front of her class and possibly up to three assessors. Then she would graduate.

It seemed strange that she would actually be celebrating happy events for a change . . . but she was also well aware that success and failure along with good and bad luck are prone to the winds of chance happenings.

'Binary pairs' was not a favourite topic for Ruby Peters, just as chance and permutations used to be the pet hates of her Eric.

# Will To Live

R uby's visit to Scotland to see her family and friends was just the best holiday she had ever had in her whole life. Robbie, Harry and the lads of the Legionnaires gave her a fun-filled week of excitement with fishing, hiking and boating on the Lochs. They now shared the same understanding that time was not to be wasted wondering if, why, how . . . it was to be lived.

There was still time to pause to remember their Eric for how he had changed into a leader and hero, always first on hand when action was required and always strong in the face of danger. He was spontaneous and had enjoyed his short time with Ruby. Robbie and Milly treated Ruby like their own daughter. Harry and Debra felt that Ruby had become too independent to be molly-coddled and drowned in idle words of sympathy. She was a hero in their eyes with a new-found drive to continue working for MI6. She had become an independent woman.

On the last day of her stay, Ruby had a few quiet words with Milly and Debra. It was strictly women's business. Things needed to be said and things needed to be acted upon by Ruby. The men were away on yet another fishing expedition.

> "Mum, Milly, I know we have all said fine words and sad words about what has happened . . . and we'll most probably grieve forever in our quiet moments and times of sadness for our Eric. He belonged to us all. But a friend of mine said that we must also carry on to prove to ourselves and to those we have lost, that we will honour their name by being stronger," said Ruby quietly whilst touching their shoulders.

> "Aye lassie, they are fine words indeed . . . and I'm sure Eric would agree with you. We are much older than you and yet we have not seen half as much loss and suffering as you have yourself, in such a short space of time," said her Mum.

> "Yes I'm of the same mind Ruby. We miss Eric so terribly but we can't bring him back. Now we know that the person who did this has been killed too . . . such a waste of life. Now what is on your mind love? . . . I'm sure you have something else that may need a wise word or two from your mums so long as we have the answers," added Milly.

Ruby smiled at them, taking two long white envelopes out of her handbag.

> "Now then, promise me you will not open these envelopes until I have left for London. Call it a game if you like . . . or call it what you will. It is something from me and Eric . . . something that I talked with him about when we were in London. It's just a letter we both wrote . . . and his signature is on there as well. So, don't open it until I'm away . . . I don't want to be crying again for a while," laughed Ruby, tearing up and turning away.

Milly and Debra looked at each other suspiciously.

"Aye, fine then. You can count on us being quiet about it until you go. You always were quite . . . dramatic," said Debra as Ruby walked hurriedly out of the room.

"Oh, it's probably something a bit private . . . maybe they were going to get married . . . oh, poor child," added Milly sadly.

They both teared up and noisily pretended to tidy up around them, each with a faint smile and similar thoughts of what could have been. Ruby had already packed her cases into the car ready for the trip back to London. She tooted the horn to indicate that she was going before negotiating her way carefully out of the tight turning circle.

Robbie, Harry and the lads were coming up the long winding driveway and stopped beside her. She smiled at them, all looking so healthy and invigorated by their fishing trip.

"You off already love?" asked Harry.

"Yes dad. Some people have to work you know. Did you catch anything bigger than that tadpole from the other day?"

"Just a few nice salmon for our tea love. We'll miss you heaps. I hope you can see us again soon. We'll be making plans to start up again . . . now that we are all free again thanks to you," shouted Robbie with a laugh.

"Aye, and how many fish did you catch then?" joked Harry.

They all looked at each other and exchanged some quite useless banter about the rain and the cold and that one of the lads had hooked his toe whilst casting, but it was time to go.

"Look after yourselves. I'll miss you so much and will be thinking about you all the time," shouted Ruby as she set off again amidst a lot of shouting and waving which faded off the further she went.

Ruby took a deep breath. It was the breath of a free woman who had nearly drowned in a sea of dark humanity. She put her foot down flat to the floor and felt the wind in her hair and the renewed life in her refreshed body.

"London in six hours!" she shouted aloud to the fresh country air.

Back at the house, the men were still talking about how Ruby was such an inspiration for them all to live life well. They had certainly had a new start themselves after being holed up at the house, enjoying the basics of life in the glorious Scottish countryside. Robbie displayed the collection of small fish to Milly and Debra who praised them for another successful catch.

"Harry, Robbie . . . Come over here. Our Ruby has given us two envelopes addressed to each of our families. She said it is a letter signed by her and Eric . . . so we can open them now she has departed. Those were her exact words," said Milly.

Robbie and Harry looked surprised.

"We've just passed the girl right now, on the road, not five minutes ago," said Robbie surprised.

"Aye and she didn't say nothing about any letters at all," added Harry, "Nothing at all."

"Well she's your daughter alright Harry. Like two peas . . . always a mystery and a quiet nod or two, to say what would require an entire book by some folk," said Debra with a grin.

"So let's be seeing what the letters say then," whispered Milly as she started tearing the side of the envelope with her thumbnail.

When they had finished, both Milly and Debra looked gobsmacked.

> "Cat got your tongue woman? . . . Come on speak up. It must be more serious than a parking fine or a stern letter from their teacher . . . Aye, we've had a few of those with our Ruby over the years," shouted Harry nervously to Debra.

Debra and Milly showed each other their letters. They were identical. They started sniffling. Harry and Robbie were on the edge of their seats with their mouths open as Debra began to explain the contents, handing over her letter to Harry as she started crying again.

> "This letter is from Ruby and Eric, and signed by both at the bottom, dated not many weeks ago . . . and . . . and they have given each of us a cheque for one hundred thousand pounds."

Robbie grabbed their letter from Milly.

> "As payment . . . as payment for your share of the four diamonds that we sold recently. In appreciation of your love and trust in bringing us up to be proud . . . independent and strong people with a sense of adventure and . . . with admiration for your . . . help and advice over the last . . . nineteen years," sobbed a shaking Robbie who had now dropped the letter.

> "Aye, we all need a stiff drink after that . . . or two . . . oh hell man, get that damn bottle over here," strained Harry trying to compose himself again.

The gathering had changed from sadness to one of hope for a better deal in their turbulent lives. Anyone could tell that they had Eric on their minds. He would have liked to have seen this day . . . and to have shared it with his Ruby.

On the road to London, Ruby was imagining with a tinge of sadness, that her 'Ruby and Eric letters' had put both families back on track to where they had been long before being ambushed by dark faceless figures - derailed from their decent and honest living. The letters were indeed a 'will' . . . a will to live life without fear.

Her thoughts were interrupted as she quickly pulled over to read a text message from Lawrence:

> "She said YES! Wedding likely for November 18th when registry office has an opening at 10am."

Ruby sent back her happy feelings:

> "Congratulations Larry. Leave the rest to me. Rosie can tell registry office of special requests and reception details. I'll look after everything after that. Best news! Did she tell you I used to call her 'Blizzard Face' because of her surname of Winters;)"

Larry's reply was simple:

> "She used to call you 'Rubber Beepers' – ha ha;) She also taught mum how to 'Ruby Kick' the old man in the leg too."

Ruby did not know whether to laugh or feel humiliated, knowing that all her classmates at school had been calling her 'Rubber Beepers' for years. No wonder she used to hear 'Beep! Beep!' noises during class and a chorus of sniggers whenever she answered a question. It was really quite funny that she didn't know about her nickname, but not at the time.

Oh, and her poor Eric. She remembered the wake-up day when he had slapped her face in protest at her silly kicking habit. She nodded and smiled at her imaginary Eric and thought of David Rowbotham hobbling around Rosie's house.

What was that damn noise? She could hear a beeping noise. Was it in her head? It was her passenger seat belt warning which had identified a package as a person. She moved it quickly. That was freaky. She laughed aloud, continuing her journey.

The company had rented Ruby a nice new unit near to Vauxhall Cross with a concierge and twenty-four hour security. To top that off, the building also housed one of her more affluent fellow classmates. Then there was the secure off-street parking for her Suzuki in a nice gated car park. She had nicknamed the car 'Max' after the bunnies in 'Max and Ruby', a TV show where they 'go through life together, share love, friendship and playtime'. It had a simple opening theme song that she would sing when she was happy.

Other motorists must have thought it quite strange to see this crazy woman bouncing around in her little car, singing out at the top of her voice.

Ruby pulled in to the underground parking lane of her building, noticing the red sign 'Redmond Place'.

Red Monde or red world, what an appropriate place to stay for a Ruby Lady she thought, as she struggled to find out exactly which of the five buttons on the key tag to press. Was this another silly psych test with hidden cameras she thought as she struggled to find the right combination. She laughed again, looking to see if anyone was watching.

The same tag was also security-coded for her unit door and the lift, giving her immediate protection . . . as soon as she could open that huge security gate. Finally, the gate glided open smoothly and quietly. She drove through slowly in search of car bay 42, which coincided with her unit number two, on the fourth floor. The other cars looked a might rather expensive compared to her tiny Suzuki: Mercedes, BMW, Lexus . . . a Lamborghini!

Ruby was forming the opinion that the company had subsidised her rent quite a bit in order to keep her safe whilst she was at home. 'Home' sounded rather nice and lazy to her, until snippets of Eric would try to intervene, muddying the pleasant images of her opinion into edginess. Her aim was to persist in her efforts to make her new life fit in with her present circumstances.

She was free, safe and was about to graduate within MI6 to official status as a 'Field Intelligence Operator – Grade 5'. She was surprised that the grades start out high and work their way up to Grade 1, but she thought that Grade 5 sounded more senior. Then she saw her parking bay.

Number 42 was a nice bay at the side of the building with only one other car parked next to her. It was a shiny burgundy Jaguar with mag wheels and a sticker on the back window reading 'Ruby Red'. Ruby did not like coincidences.

As she was getting out of the car, the door of the Jaguar opened and a young man eased himself out. His blue shirt and light trousers suited his tall frame. A jacket grabbed from the car casually thrown over his left shoulder appeared neatly pressed. He inched backwards into the laneway. Was that Dunlop Volley Classic sports shoes on his feet? All the rage with pop stars and writers she remembered.

Ruby's quick assessment of the man, before he had even spoken had already placed this man as a writer . . . or creative artist. Maybe even a musician or film composer. 'Ruby Red' was probably where he would dine in between jet-setting all around the world, or it could be . . .

"Hello there! You're new here aren't you?" he asked kindly.

"Yes, hello, I'm Ruby. Ruby Peters and I've just moved in to unit 42. Well today is in fact my first day here," she replied looking at his surprised face.

"Ruby, well, fancy that. My advertising company is called 'Ruby Red'. See here on this sticker. I make up your mind on what you want . . . err with things you buy. Well, sort of," he added vaguely, pointing at the sticker whilst smiling at her face, giving away an automatic quick glance at the rest of her whilst trying to stay focussed on what he was saying.

"That may not work with me I'm afraid . . . err?"

"Oh sorry, I'm Reddy," he replied enthusiastically with a wink.

"Really!" she retorted shaking her head with a sigh.

"Yes . . . Andrew Reddy. I'm sorry Ruby, I always like doing that. Rather childish I know, but it seems to have stuck with me forever," he replied with a grin.

Ruby laughed. What a strange fellow this was.

"It's almost like your tag line in an advertising product. I will have to think of one for myself," she joked.

"Yes, how clever. I never thought of it like that. Now then, let me see . . . your tag line could be . . . well, I don't know what you do, do I?"

"Oh I'm a . . . an interpreter at the Foreign Office . . . just reading and writing and foreign investments. You know . . . just the usual stuff."

Andrew rubbed his chin, thought for a while and then launched into his dramatic tag line for Ruby, complete with wide arm movements.

"I have 'Where your letters are carefully Ruby Read' or 'Make your day a Ruby Red Letter Day'. Did you know that a Red Letter day is called a Scarlett Day in academia by the way?"

"Well no, but Scarlett is my family nickname Andrew. How fascinating is that."

They both laughed. Ruby felt quite at ease with her new friend.

"Must go Ruby, I've got to get ready for an interview with a client. It would be nice to catch up with you sometime. I think we would get on really well . . . if you don't mind my calling on you. Or, I may see you at your car again," he offered excitedly.

"Max and I would love that Andrew," she replied with a grin.

"Oh sorry, again, I never thought to ask you if you were single, err available . . . I mean with someone," he stammered.

Ruby sighed and shook her head. She scrunched up her nose as she reconsidered.

"I'm sorry Andrew, I always like doing that. Rather childish I know, but it seems to have stuck with me forever. Max is the name of my car . . . and yes, it would be so nice to see you again. Maybe for a coffee or . . . "

"Gosh! My heart is in my throat Ruby. I'm not usually so adventurous when I meet a girl, but this time I just wanted to go all out . . . I mean . . . well anyway, goodbye for now."

Andrew nearly fell over himself as he avoided walking into the side wall of the parking bay. He headed towards the small private storage door with the number 60. Ruby could see the door open automatically and various boxes and signage was on show.

She walked towards the lift and pressed all five buttons, one after the other. After a few seconds of silence, she could hear the car park door opening behind her, but nothing else.

A quick glance above the lift door showed that it was currently at level one and still descending. Then suddenly the lift door opened and a woman in a green business suit caught her gaze as she smiled and said hello, before walking towards the other end of the car park.

The lift was quite fast. It was also quiet and warm with a gentle theme playing in the background. Ruby recognised it as 'Milonga del Angel' being played as a saxophone and piano duet against a moving orchestral background. She had loved that piece after first hearing it played by her friend Susan at music school on one particular Saturday.

Ruby thought that Susan would still be at the Conservatorium of Music and made a mental note about contacting her to see what she was doing. Then she remembered Susan's words of advice on how she herself had coped with sadness and that constant dreaming about those romantic ideas that always seemed beyond her reach:

> "Let the music smooth out your fears. Let it caress your feelings into submission. Let your heart and mind become one . . . and you will never be sad for long . . . or alone with your troubles."

She loved Susan's soft lilting Irish accent. She was from Cork. Susan Annette O'Brien was her one true friend when such a friend was very much, desperately needed. They even had a pact at school that whoever would be rich and famous first would search out and send for the other . . . to ground them back into reality and to reconnect their close friendship. They did not like posers like 'Blizzard Face' and her following.

She would joke that she was the first one to have 'sax', which would have them giggling in class at every opportunity. The other gem of wisdom was that Susan's initials spelt out the name of a popular biscuit. She was always eating them, dropping crumbs all around her, leaving a noticeable trail throughout the school, leading to her scruffy desk.

Life was so clear and free when they were together, when they were young and innocent – well apart from their tricks played on poor Mister James, the science teacher. The school itself however was really a somewhat cold and disheartening throwback to Victorian times where rule of might swayed logic and care for others. It was a nice feeling to be free of such an institution.

Ruby laughed to herself at some of her earlier thoughts and ideas on life. Now she was in MI6 as a spy with a rather courageous record of accomplishment.

> "Who would have thought Eric?" she whispered softly, "and whoever knows what is to come . . . from what has passed?"

# Magic Happens

Ruby had settled in to Redmond Place with ease. She felt that it was like partly reaching up to touch the sky when looking through the window . . . which it did on an especially cold and misty day.

The balcony was a relaxing haven for those quiet drinks with friends — especially that nice evening with Andrew. They were working opposing hours and separated by distance during the week due to Andrew's advertising campaigns but she found herself looking forward to his return.

She had always promised herself that she needed to get out more, to meet new people and not hide away when she was not working. So far, she knew at least there was some progress in her ability to cope with the closer company of others, realising that she really enjoyed life after all, as long as she could control the highs and lows of her anxiety.

Andrew was so very calm and understanding of her simple needs, without having to ask her any personal questions or make her feel threatened by his obvious growing affection for her. A gentle kiss secreted after their last evening of music and a few drinks, had Andrew lingering on her lips as he held her close. Ruby felt as if she had been touched by an angel. He had drawn her into a soft embrace with the lightness and warmth of a spring day. She missed such feelings of closeness.

It was a different intensity to what she had shared with Eric. This had made her feel strange inside . . . a nice feeling of belonging, but combined with at least the hint of her wanting to let go of Eric's weakening influence on her emotions.

Ruby's other interest was in keeping her promise with Larry and Rosie to look after their wedding day, based of course on the personal requirements of Rosie. Larry was easy to please. Another text had come through from Larry just one week out from his defining day:

> "Confirm service starts at 10am Saturday. Reception goes from 11am to 1pm. You said to pack for 2 days. Don't know where we're going at all Ruby;) Rosie knows nothing (especially today) Ha Ha. Larry."

Ruby replied short and to the point:

> "Just be there BEFORE 10am Larry. Then relax and let me take care of everything else. Best wishes to you all - Ruby."

She had been planning this wedding as if it was her own. There was a glint in her eye as she worked through the logistics of the event in her mind, putting pen to paper to write down the key times for each critical stage. She had also sneaked back to Doulton on one weekend to spy on Rosie and Larry to see what they were really like.

They loved their children to bits and their home life was seemingly much improved. Rosie's stepfather appeared to have smartened himself up for the coming event, even buying a new suit in town after having a haircut and treating himself and his wife Beryl to a nice lunch.

Beryl had a new sense of pride now that her daughter with two kids in tow was tying the knot with a good catch. It was like something magical was happening to them all, something that had always been there somewhere but had been beyond their grasp, until focussed by this wedding.

The children, baby David and Little Ruby were real eye-catchers and played up to anyone gullible enough to share their enthusiasm for making an absolute mess and having fun.

And Ruby . . . this was not only her project for work, bordering on a religious miracle, but something that had enriched her life. Well, they did say that was what it was for, but even MI6 couldn't have imagined the impact it would have on their star student, transformed into a firm believer in faith . . . 'believe and it shall be done'. Certainly, changing 'Blizzard Face' into 'Snow White' could just be sheer blind faith. Yet, it was happening before her eyes.

As the day wore on and Ruby was still considering whether to call Andrew, there was a knock on the door. It was so slight that she may have missed it. She walked to the door wondering who it could be, hoping that it was not Deidre from down the hall, who was always wanting her to join her knitting club. Knitting indeed! She had to look it up on her computer to see what sorts of mess she could get herself into, probably turning the session into one that could be described as getting knotted.

As the door opened, she sensed it was Andrew. Her heart started beating faster. Trying to clear the lump from her throat, she stared through a mist at Andrew but could not say a word.

He looked at her with that smile. She was drowning in that deep blueness of his eyes, until he took her hand gently, then came very close, to kiss her lightly.

"Come in Andrew, I was hoping that it was you," she said.

"I've missed you all this last week Ruby. I've been thinking about you throughout all my waking hours and have come to realise that I have always missed you . . . even before I met you."

Andrew handed over the flowers that somehow Ruby had missed seeing. She smiled. This was almost too old school.

"Thanks Andrew, they're lovely . . . I have missed you too."

They went out onto the balcony where the trees were still shedding their golden leaves onto the street below. The late sun outlined the branches of the silver birch and oak trees with an orange glow.

"Oh, there was one thing I wanted to ask you. I'm planning a wedding over the weekend and . . ."

"Wow, that was sudden!" he choked.

They both laughed as he started to open the bottle of wine that he had also brought. No, she hadn't seen that either although it was in the same hand as the flowers – in a red bag!

"No, this wedding is for a friend of mine. It's a long story Andrew but I would like to ask if you would join me on this Saturday. Short notice I know, but I have been planning it as part of a work project. It's . . . it's in Doulton."

Andrew did not hesitate, relieving Ruby from her own spontaneous emotional outburst. What was she thinking . . . so soon?

"I'd love to take you to a wedding Ruby . . . anybody's wedding, or christening . . . even a funeral or two just to be with you for a while . . . and the further the better," he joked kindly.

Ruby was very happy that he would be there but the ghost within her told her differently. They both knew that they would have to stay overnight.

Ruby and probably Andrew were now both wondering if the awkward details could work themselves out to give each other their options.

"I may have to leave you for short spells just to confirm that certain people have arrived, you know, the one's I've planned to turn up, if that's alright."

"Sure that's absolutely fine. So what have you got planned?" he asked with interest.

Ruby concentrated on the event and welled up with excitement as she snatched the list from the table to show him . . . then suddenly pulled it away from him.

"No Andrew. It will be such a special day that I want you to be as much surprised as everyone else will be," she gushed, uncertain of her impulsive defence.

"Oh I'll be in heaven alright. Now how can that be a work project Ruby? What's it all about? It sounds a bit whacky if you're organising someone's wedding to score points at work."

Ruby scrunched up her nose and started to explain.

"As the last part of my graduation process, they found someone that I used to hate and I have to find out how to improve or benefit their lives . . . all without them knowing mind you . . . and then verify that my project had the right positive effects on them before completing my report," gushed Ruby, ending in a 'hey presto' look.

Andrew looked bewildered at first but appeared to be warming to this strange new idea of helping someone you hate.

It could actually be a good advertising campaign idea for a client.

> "And who did you hate so bad, that you must now help them?"

> "Blizzard Face," she blurted.

> "Blizzard Face? Now that's what I call a picture of hate. I just hope that she appreciates your helping hand as a gift rather than someone trying to wreck her special day. Well, I know you wouldn't but let's face it, can a 'Blizzard Face' change its icy spots?" he asked.

> "Real name is Rosemary Winters. She turns out of course to be a really nice person with two children who . . . wait for it, drum roll . . . she has named her daughter after me!"

> "Wow, you wouldn't read about it. Well, you just might if you pull it off. And did she have a name for you too?"

> "Oh no, she didn't. Not that I know of anyway," replied Ruby abruptly.

Andrew just stared at Ruby with a grin that just kept getting wider, in stages, making her more embarrassed.

> "Oh, OK then. It was 'Rubber Beepers'. Yes, I know as in 'Beep! Beep! Very funny . . . and I never knew for years it seems."

As they both laughed out aloud, it was obvious that they were drifting closer. It had gelled somewhere in between Andrew accepting her wedding invitation and Ruby making the sound of a reversing truck.

As Andrew left Ruby's unit there was a panic as to what stage they were both comfortable with in their relationship with the embracing goodbyes. In the end, they both stuffed up, overthinking thoughts about their weekend away, leading to a fumbling of arms and hands and noses until they were left with a light kiss and bewildered looks of longing and regret.

After she had closed the door and returned to the lounge area, it dawned on her that she was 'in a relationship' and that the wedding day was going to be one hell of a day for everyone . . . EVERYONE!

Ruby ran over to her extensive itinerary for the day and looked at the list of participants and the venues with arranged entertainment and the transport logistics. She thought that she would be well suited to being a director in a movie, before realising that she was in fact filling that very same role in the wedding extravaganza of the decade . . . at least for the likes of Doulton anyway.

In her anticipation of Andrew visiting, she had not opened up the package that had arrived. It was about the size of a greeting card. She opened it carefully and welcomed the contents with a look of both surprise and pride. Susan had sent a DVD of her recording with the London Philharmonic Orchestra.

She scrunched up her nose and headed for the fridge where another bottle of Riccadonna sparkling wine was icy cold. She placed the DVD into the player which started automatically and then poured a fresh glass of wine as the first track played.

'Milonga del Angel' with the magical sound of Susan's unmistakable saxophone glided effortlessly through the slides and nuances of this exciting piece of music.

Ruby had spoken to Susan only a few days earlier and had spent an entire hour catching up with all that had happened in her life since they had left school. Ruby had made an effort to sketch out and play down some of the events that had changed her life. And now, there was Andrew she could add to any conversation, almost like having a baby or a pet to roll out at uncomfortable moments in conversation. Although Andrew was neither, he did get a mention . . . once or twice.

Susan was in Paris but said she would attend the wedding to play just 'a small piece', to create an atmosphere of love for the wedding ceremony. Everything was set for a beautiful wedding, but thoughts about Andrew were making her anxious, alternating between staying with him over a weekend and whether she was even ready to start dating again.

The outcome could end up being perfect or become the final tipping point of her sanity. It could bring everything undone. Her ability to keep living was fraught with the prospect of indecision and her memories kept throwing up obstacles.

She sipped the wine slowly with eyes closed, taking in the melancholy tones of 'Les Moulins de Mon Coeur', as she imagined Andrew flying his glider in the clear summer sky as she looked upwards, understanding that he was thinking of her.

It was that innermost knowing only lovers can sense even when apart, that made her wish Andrew was holding her close.

There was a loud knock at the door, which startled her.

She opened it slowly, expectantly.

He grabbed her forcefully, pulling her close, giving her a long kiss that was urgently accepted.

She slowly stepped back as he carried her weight with his embrace as if floating with the swirl of the music, sharing their closeness without a word spoken between them.

The door had closed. There was no turning back now.

# That Weekend

R uby had set off for Doulton early on the Friday afternoon to make sure that everything was ready for the Saturday morning wedding. It was a pleasant enough trip. She arrived tired but able to check that the registry office was fully prepared for what she had planned. There were so many nice understanding people willing to make sure that the timing and effects would be just perfect.

The reception venue had been kept as secret as possible for a small town. Although that in itself was reason enough for the secret to leak out, Rosie and Larry had not to found out. The venue organisers and their staff had been very understanding and secretive.

Andrew had cancelled all his appointments for the weekend so that he could meet Ruby in time for the start of the Wedding reception. He was looking forward to being with her again. He had texted her several times with messages of support and love during the week . . . that was up to Thursday. He was due to arrive in time for the reception because of an unseen business appointment. He had called it his reward from a happy customer.

Ruby's Friday evening was spent talking to Larry on the phone explaining the timing of all the events but not the location of the reception.

> "Remember to keep Rosie from leaving the registry office until someone comes in to take you to the reception. OK? From then on, everything has been organised. So you can concentrate on looking after your new wife . . . to enjoy a special day."

> "Why does she have to stay inside until you signal?" he had asked.

> "Because there will be some activity outside that needs to be kept secret until you both come out together. Leave it to me Larry. Everything is going to be great," she replied.

Larry sounded a bit unsure as to why he was so trusting of someone who once hated his 'Blizzard Face'. But now it was too late. The initial reason for trusting her was that Ruby was paying for everything. Now, he thought that he should have done a bit more checking.

> "I'm totally trusting in you Ruby. If anything happens and my Rosie gets hurt in any way . . . well I won't be too pleased. I think that my eyes have been bigger than my wallet . . . I mean I would probably have put the wedding off until I was more financial."

Ruby put herself in his position.

> "You will see that everything will be much more than you ever expected Larry. You know the wedding itself will be fine for a start, so you are relying on me to handle your reception. And I have checked and double-checked that every single piece of the jigsaw has come

together and many people have put themselves out to make it happen . . . just for you and Rosie."

With that, Larry seemed to be in a better mood. After all, it was his wedding the next day, when nerves are always on edge and uncertainties abound.

"Did you organise your rings to be picked up from the jeweller from the range I gave you Larry? My representative will get them on Saturday morning and give them to you before the service."

"Yes they were really nice. They look expensive though Ruby . . . how can I repay you for doing all this?" he asked.

Ruby could tell that he was close to tears.

"Just be there for Rosie. That's all the thanks anyone wants from you both."

Without doubt there were many people who didn't get much sleep that night. Saturday started for Ruby with an alarm call at six o'clock. Not that she needed it. She was already showering and singing her favourite happy song . . . "Max and Ruby, Ruby and Max".

Andrew was due to be on the road in his Jaguar coming from Liverpool. Ruby pictured him enjoying the ride with an open window and smiling at everyone and everything that came into vision. He had not called at all though which surprised her.

Larry and Rosie were looking at each other in bed, staring as if they had never seen each other before . . . and they had not in this same way. They were making their lives into a family. Little Ruby was waiting at the half-open door, peaking in to see baby brother David staring at his hanging mobile . . . as her mum and dad turned to see her innocent smile and roughed-up hair.

"Do you want to wear your new dress Ruby? We are going out today," asked Rosie.

"Why? Where are we going mummy?"

"Mummy and daddy are getting married today Ruby. Want to come and see that . . . and then we are going to have some dinner and maybe some dancing too," replied Larry.

Little Ruby just looked in amazement and tried to work out what was going on. Dinner and dancing sounded good to her.

"Can I wear my red shoes? I want my red shoes."

Larry looked at the clock. It was seven o'clock.

"Quick. Get up. Get ready. Hurry," shouted Larry in a panic.

Rosie looked at him as if he was on fire. She had never seen such enthusiasm and energy for what was to be his last day as a single man . . . with a girlfriend and two lovely children.

Little Ruby had caught on and was running up and down shouting along with her mother.

"Hurry up, hurry, it's seven o'clock. I want my red shoes. Mummy where are my red shoes?"

Larry looked stunned. He was getting married.

"We should get married every weekend. You look funny when you're in panic mode. You don't think that I would let you be late on this day do you?" said Rosie softly, catching a glimpse of the clock.

"It's gone seven o'clock. I've got to get going."

Rosie's mum and dad were also stirring.

"Are you ready for today love? Our Rosie is getting married. I never thought I'd see Rosie and Larry get married," said David.

"You know, I'm really proud of the way you've approached this Dave. Rosie's kids . . . well, and Larry too . . . they've changed this house, changed you and me. It's made for quite a happy home," replied Beryl quietly.

"I'll be the first to agree with you. I've not been the most . . . agreeable man to get along with. Probably because of my own upbringing, you know. However, we've managed to get through lass. So now, we have a wedding to go to. Let's make it a grand day for Rosie and the kids."

"And Larry?" she enquired cautiously with a smile.

"Aye he's not a bad lad that one. He's a good lad."

"I didn't think Larry could afford to get married yet, but he seems to be managing alright. I wonder what he has planned for the reception though?" asked Beryl nervously.

"He said something about a friend of Rosie's from school was handling all that. I reckon he might have won a prize or something. He doesn't seem too bothered about the planning side either. He'll do our Rosie proud. I know that," replied David.

The time of eight o'clock had other people around the town scurrying to get organised. Some people knew a little of what was going on but Ruby had not told each group who their activity was for, or who else was involved. They only knew it was a wedding day for someone special.

Rosie was attending the beauty salon surrounded by two of her friends from the old gang . . . and their noisy children.

Larry and David were putting on their new suits, both paid for by David for this most important day out.

"Thanks dad. I really appreciate what you've done for me and Rosie. We've had some earlier differences I know but I must say that you're a great bloke after all," said Larry proudly.

"Gee, steady on lad. You'll have me crying in me beer if that keeps on. Here stick this in your jacket."

David put a handkerchief into Larry's top pocket and patted him on the back. Then he got a small hip flask and secreted it into his own inside pocket with a smile at Larry.

"You've got to remember your name lad. Right then, let's get going. We should be there at nine thirty."

As they stepped outside waiting for their lift to the registry office, a shiny red Mercedes Benz stopped and the chauffeur raced around to open the door for them. Larry and David just stared at their fancy ride.

"Good morning gentlemen. I am here to take you to the registry office. My name is Tian. If you want anything, just ask. I have placed the rings inside the box, which is in front of you. I'll drive around town until I can drop you off at nine thirty."

David picked it up and opened it to show two splendid diamond rings nestling in a dark blue velvet cushion.

"By thee heck lad, did you win the lottery. These look like the one's on the rich and famous."

"I was helped by an angel dad . . . an angel," said Larry softly.

At the same time, a stretched red Mercedes limousine arrived and parked outside the beauty salon. The driver was standing next to it looking down the road.

"Wow, look at that limo Jasmine. Someone's got some money in town," said a wide-eyed Rosie to her friend.

There was a lot of chatter until the salon owner came out to give her a ruby brooch to match her navy and white outfit.

> "Just a token of friendship from the company that has paid for all you girls and yourself to be made up for the day," she said, "oh and a bunch of forget-me-nots for each of you . . . and a toy bunny for little Ruby, with her name on it."

Rosie looked surprised, astonished, embarrassed. Little Ruby was shouting and screaming for joy. Rosie had to shout out to be heard. All the other children wanted a bunny too.

> "But what company would do this for me? I don't know anyone in any company. This must be Larry's idea of a joke. I hope he can afford all this," said Rosie, now slightly annoyed.

Rosie and the girls looked at each other in amazement.

> "Apparently you will find out at the reception," she replied indicating that she may not know herself, probably because she didn't.

At the registry office, all was quiet. It was nine o'clock. The doors were carefully opened, as three staff members peeked outside to survey their quiet front entrance and car park. Suddenly four cars pulled up in succession and then a red van.

The people from all the vehicles piled out to help the van driver unload his huge collection of flowers . . . red roses. The senior officer from the registry office stared open-mouthed before rushing down to the van waving his arms frantically.

> "Excuse me. Excuse me. Sorry, but you have the wrong address. We only have a registry wedding at ten o'clock. It's not a bloody cathedral you know."

> "I've got ten o'clock for Rosie Winters and Larry Oates. There is no mistake here mate and these people here are their friends anyway. I was told to contact them last

night to give me a hand with this lot," he replied with a laugh.

Rosie and her handmaidens three, surrounded by five noisy and over-excited children were all set to go. They checked the time and it was decided they may as well have a glass of the champagne that had also arrived with 'bunny' and the attached note: 'From one bunny to another.'

David and Larry had now arrived at the registry office. They were welcomed by the staff at the door and promptly hustled into the waiting room, which was now overflowing with red flowers.

"Did you run out of garden matey?" asked David with a laugh.

"No, these are all for your wedding. Your friends helped to bring them in. They'll be back here in a minute. Oh and there's another fellow that is here to see you Mister Oates. He said that he hopes you don't mind him coming, but will understand if you want him to go away. He's waiting outside."

Larry was in a bit of a daze. "Who could it be", he thought.

"Geez, I hope it's not the debt collector sent to shake me up for all these expenses," whispered Larry to a rather worried looking David.

Larry cautiously opened the door and saw another miracle of Ruby's handy work. They looked at each other, warily at first. Tony looked at his son and smiled hesitantly. Larry approached him with a serious expression, until he got closer. Stretching out his hand, Larry nodded his head with a smile that invited friendship, which completed the surprise.

"Dad. Thanks for coming dad. It's been a while. I wanted you to come but didn't know if you would want to. And then . . ."

"You never asked Larry. I've never stopped thinking about you. I thought that you wanted to start over again with your Rosie and move on from me," he replied.

"How did you know about the wedding?" asked Larry.

"I believe you know someone called Ruby. She made all the arrangements and filled me in on your family. You have two children? Well, you seem to have done very well for yourself son. A degree, a job, children and soon a lovely wife who I only knew as that schoolgirl called Rosemary. Congratulations son."

Larry was beside himself. Was he dreaming all this or had all the planets lined up to shower him with the things he had only dreamed were possible?

"Wait there a minute dad. I want you to meet someone."

Larry rushed back to the waiting room where David was talking with Larry's friends. He froze up thinking how Dave would handle all this after being such a great replacement dad.

"Dave, I've got someone for you to meet. It's my dad. I know that you may not want to see him, but that's ok by me."

David put his hand on Larry's shoulder.

"We've already met lad. I knew he was coming today. We met through one of your friends who invited me and your dad to a few drinks in town a few weeks ago. Sure, we sorted some stuff out together and decided that it was your day and that you should have him there. That friend of yours is mighty convincing lad. She told us not to say anything until today."

"She? Well then I think I know the particular girl in question. Our daughter is named after her. Rosie and Ruby used to hate each other to blazes and . . . oh no, I hope Rosie is ok with all this. She doesn't know anything about this you know. You would think that they would get on now they are older . . . but girls may have a different perspective than us. If I had told her about Ruby, it will ruin the surprise and Ruby made me promise not to tell her. She's the one who has organised and paid for everything," said Larry.

"Blimey she must be really rich boy," exclaimed Tony.

"Only in what she does dad. Her company may be paying, but she has put everything into this one day . . . me and Rosie's day."

Over at the salon, the driver of the Mercedes had put on his hat and walked towards the salon door much to the astonishment of Rosie and her party.

"Good morning ladies. Your ride awaits you for the journey to the registry office in town. A Mister Lawrence Oates awaits your pleasure. You will find a glass of champagne near your seat and a soft-drink for the children."

Rosie was speechless. Eventually they all started to chat rapidly at all the fuss being made over Rosie.

"That car is red like my red shoes," screamed little Ruby.

Rosie was thinking about the cost, but the driver already seeing that Rosie looked a little worried about the size of the event, had a quiet word to her, pulling her to one side.

"Miss Rosie, I was told to tell you not to worry about any cost of what you see tonight as it is all fully paid. Your 'husband to be' has been told the same thing. Think of it as being a prize. You will meet the person who has organised all this at the reception and that person says that they hope you will make friends, as you have made friends with others."

"But who is it?"

The driver shook his head and smiled, offering to help Rosie into the limousine. The journey was noisy except for Rosie wondering who had done this for her and Larry. The limousine glided into the car park as Larry, David and Tony looked out of the window.

"Oh, my god, will you look at that," said Larry shaking his head, "She must have totally lost her mind."

Tian was filming the event discreetly now as official photographer, carefully arranging the group photo of the bride and her friends leaving the stretch limo. The guests inside were interrupted by the registry officer.

"It's now five minutes to ten o'clock and the bride and her party have arrived for the service and signing. Please make your way to the main room."

Everyone ran in to greet each other amid the noise of screaming children, and with the bride and her party now a little tipsy after their second glass of champagne. Rosie and Larry slowly walked towards each other and hugged each other before kissing. Rosie kept him close.

"Larry, how can we afford all this? Did you win a prize and not tell me? You did, didn't you, you scallywag."

Larry just smiled and looked towards his daughter playing with her new bunny. Then he whispered to Rosie.

"The signature of the person who did all this is evident in everything that has been supplied. The cars for instance, your brooch . . . even a little bunny. And to top that off love, I want to introduce you to . . . my father, Tony."

Larry swung around. Rosie saw Larry's only trace of family.

"Rosie this is Tony Oates, my father. Dad this is Rosie Winters soon to become Mrs Rosie Oates . . . my wife."

Tony reached out for her hand and then Rosie raced forwards to give him a hug.

"This is surely a magic day. A lot of thought has gone into this. I still don't know who is responsible."

"You will meet that person at the reception love. You will be surprised . . . and then maybe not so surprised at all," said Larry.

"I love your children Rosie. You look absolutely beautiful and I'm just so very happy to share with you, your special day," said Tony.

"Look daddy, I've got a rabbit. Look. Look it is called Ruby just like me," shouted little Ruby, pointing to the nametag.

Rosie thought about Ruby Peters . . . and her boyfriend Eric, who had died in Dogbol not a month ago.

"Larry, we should have invited Ruby Peters to our wedding. She has had some hard times. Oh, we should have contacted her somehow," said Rosie sadly.

Larry looked at her and thought about how the hatred between the two of them had blown up out of all proportion. It was only a schoolyard spat after all, and Rosie had changed her mind about Ruby a long time ago.

"Yes, she had her house destroyed a while back didn't she?" said Larry.

"And her poor Eric was murdered by a maniac. I heard about it in the salon today and could not believe it. You would have known Eric Johnson wouldn't you?"

Larry was stunned that Ruby had not told him. He looked ashen and turned away. Rosie was about to comfort him when the registry officer brought their wedding to order. She held Larry's hand until he recovered and focussed on his wedding.

Rosie had never seen Larry so emotional as this.

The service went according to plan but when the rings were presented to each other, they were astonished at the size of the rings. They must have been switched for more expensive versions of the ones they had chosen, surely. They glistened and sparkled and fitted perfectly.

> "I now pronounce you husband and wife. Please feel free to kiss the bride at your pleasure . . . and I'm talking to her new husband here," said the officer with a huge smile.

There were cheers and shouting, crying and hugging and kissing. The children thought it was a giant party. The official photographer was very pleased with the photos he had taken. One was of the huge face of a bunny, which had been thrust into the arranged shot of the bridal party.

Tian came to the door dressed in a red dress and wearing a ruby brooch to make an announcement.

> "If you please everyone, if I can I have your attention please? Your transport to the reception is waiting outside. If everyone can make their way outside now please . . . but a few photos first are in order first I think."

They all piled outside, each one staring at the huge red coach that was taking up half the car park. There were people already inside. The red Mercedes cars had gone.

After the photos were taken, the party started boarding the bus. It was no ordinary bus ride. This one had music – live music. It had a ten-piece orchestra playing. There were violin players, and a synthesiser piano, a saxophone and cello and a conductor all dressed in red. The first piece of music that they played was 'Milonga Del Angel'.

The conductor was a woman. When she turned around quickly every now and again, they could see that she was wearing a tall hat with woolly red hair stuck to the sides and . . .

a moustache. On each seat was a programme of the music, which they would play until they reached reception and during the start of the reception. It read like a dinner menu, starting with some classical, then jazz and finally some dance music.

The list of players read like a who's who of the London Philharmonic Orchestra with the saxophonist being Susan Annette O'Brien who was floating notes across the registers as if they were clouds in the sky.

Everyone set in for a luxurious ride with beautiful music and another glass of champagne.

"Where are we going Larry?" asked an excited Rosie and some of the other guests.

Larry looked as surprised as the rest of them when he replied rather embarrassed and making things a bit surreal.

"I haven't a clue. I never asked about that bit."

"Oh Larry, you always were one for attention to detail," said Rosie, busily flashing her sparkling new ring to her mum.

Larry went up to the conductor and whispered quietly.

"It's OK Ruby. She told me that she should have invited you to the wedding just now. So, everything will be fine. You have done a magnificent job today. Everyone is so happy and excited about all the unexpected things that keep happening."

"It's not over yet my boy," said Ruby twirling her moustache.

The bus kept going . . . and going until people were starting to worry about exactly how far this reception venue was in relation to the city of Doulton.

As they drove out of the city, the spectacular site of the new golf course convention centre called the 'Western Oasis' appeared into view. The front gate had a sign that read 'Congratulations Rosie and Larry' written in thick red paint.

The bus glided to a stop at the main entrance to the reception bay where two concierges dressed in red suits swiftly stood by the bus to welcome their guests. There was another man standing at the entrance looking rather worse for wear. He was holding two glasses of champagne and looked very much at ease. His coat was ruffled and his hair was untidy.

Ruby ushered everyone off the bus as she stared at his antics. There was a round of applause for the musicians who appeared extremely happy to be part of the event.

The man walked up to Ruby who was now becoming very embarrassed for him. He looked as if he had been drinking at the hotel for quite a while. Andrew was drunk, now spilling wine from the glasses.

> "I'm waiting for a gem of a woman. She's about your height and goes by the name of . . ." he said slurring his words.

Just then, completely unscripted and perfectly timed, the bus started to reverse to enable it to travel to the waiting bay.

'Beep, Beep, Beep'

Andrew and Larry laughed out aloud, catching the gaze of Rosie who looked at Ruby, then at the red bus, the orchestra and her little Ruby's new toy rabbit.

> "Ruby Peters, well I never, it is you behind that moustache isn't it? You are the one person that I have always wanted to catch up with but thought that maybe you didn't like me much at all," cried Rosie rushing towards her.

They had a long hug and looked at each other with big smiles, while a concierge rushed in to save two glasses from smashing into the floor next to the entrance.

"It was the sound of the reversing bus that gave me away wasn't it? That wasn't even planned you know."

"So what's this all about then? Come on. You've gone completely over the top with this. The cars, the rings, the bus with an orchestra, the reception . . . it's all so fantastic . . . but why? A phone call would have worked too you know."

Andrew poked his head around Ruby's waist to say a few words to Rosie.

"Hello. 'Rubber Beeper' meet 'Blizzard Face'. Hi, I'm Andrew and I am ready."

Larry nearly fell over with laughter.

"Oh, Andrew that's not very nice. That's all in the past. It was at school. That is very rude. You're drunk!" said Ruby annoyed, watching him sway around.

Rosie made light of it, fending off Andrew's attempt to hug her, with Larry catching him mid fall.

"I think it's so funny Ruby. It's hilarious that we both got caught up in different sides at school and couldn't find a way to be friends . . . until now. So come on, tell me what this is all about or else I'll kick you in the shin," joked Rosie, forgetting that her comment would bring up thoughts about Eric.

She put her arm around Ruby and spoke quietly.

"You can tell me about Eric later, but only if you want to . . . I am so very sorry."

Ruby looked at her and smiled.

"Thank you Rosie. I'm getting over it now. It's time to move ahead . . . and look we're here to celebrate your wedding. So let's get in there and have a ball. I'll tell you all about why I did all this if you promise to stay friends . . . now that we have caught up. And tell me about little

Ruby over there. She's so nice and sweet . . . not like I used to be."

As they were going through the front revolving doors, a skimpy looking waif of a girl with untidy hair brushed past them, touching Andrew and giving him one of those amorous looks.

"Bye love. We must do it again soon love."

They were the fateful words that sealed Andrew's demise.

Ruby looked at him with disgust before turning to join her party. She looked back at the startled wedding party then back at Andrew.

"Go home Andrew. I don't want to see you ever again."

Rosie and Larry were also working out what was going on.

"Loser," whispered Larry as he walked past Andrew.

Rosie was more definite. Andrew reeled back on one leg. He clutched the shin of his other leg before falling over. It looked like he was going to make as scene as anger welled from within. As he stood up to re-enter the hotel, a firm hand on his shoulder from a lady in a red dress brought him instant pain. He thought he was going to die.

"If you're not out of here in ten seconds, I'm going to break your neck and then get my colleagues over there to throw your worthless body into the river. Got it? Don't ever show your face to Ruby again . . . or you will see us again very quickly. You won't get off lightly if there is a next time," she said pointing out the two hefty members of her team that she had organised to cover the event.

Andrew looked scared and hobbled off to the car park. The two men followed him to make sure that he drove away. Andrew had met his match with a worldly-wise woman.

Meanwhile, in the foyer, Ruby was entertained by a funny moment to make her feel better.

> "Ah, Miss Dee Plant, it's so nice of you to attend the wedding," said David with a grin.

> "Dee Plant? This is Ruby Peters . . . the one I named little Ruby after. She has organised all of this," queried Rosie.

> "Yes well, it was just part of the research Rosie that I fronted up to David as Claret De Plant on account that I couldn't talk to you directly before the event. And I then I also wanted to get Larry's father here for his wedding," explained Ruby.

> "That's right love, Ruby here organised my meeting with Larry's father at the pub where she told me who she really was. That's how I met Tony. It was all arranged so that there would be no awkward moments on the day," added David.

The hotel had set aside a nice area for the reception with red tablecloths and napkins and an ice sculpture of a mermaid with a distinctive pink tinge. It was an evening of fine dining and music that seemed to please all the hotel staff as they watched, wondering who these people were to have managed such a spectacular event.

Tian and her two minders patrolled the event until Ruby, Rosie and Larry and their friends and family had finished up in their rooms for the night.

Ruby had the chance to talk about her project and that they were all lucky to be the beneficiaries of her company policy of making such projects a rite of passage for all new recruits. Rosie and Larry thought it was great that Ruby's company had chosen Rosie to be her 'used to be hated' subject.

There was just one more bit of magic that Ruby had managed to deliver after much persuading over a few personal visits. When Rosie and Larry finally went up to their room for the next two days of pampering, they noticed an envelope on the bed. It was addressed to Rosie.

She opened it and found a letter and a photograph. Larry watched her reaction as she looked at the photo and started crying. As he put his arm around her, she gave him the photo and started to read the letter.

> "That's me Larry. That's me when I was six . . . and my mum . . . and my dad before he was killed. But then how am I reading his letter?"

Larry stared at the tough looking man with a gentle smile on his face. He was holding Rosie on his knee who was laughing. Beryl had her arm around this man. They looked like a real family. Larry had been told by Ruby that Rosie's dad had a violent quick temper if he was annoyed with someone . . . but that most of the time he was a very quiet loving man.

> "What does it say Rosie," he asked quietly.

> "It's from my dad Larry. He wishes us both well. He says he is sorry for leaving mum and me to fend for ourselves . . . he went to prison! I didn't know that. He says he has been following my life from inside . . . the schools, the children . . . and you Larry. He says that I am blessed with having a good man to provide for me and the children . . . something that he could not do himself. He says he was framed and that he did not do the crime. He signs it 'Love from your proud dad' and an address if I want to send him a letter back."

Rosie and Larry hugged each other and did not say another word as they looked in on baby David and little Ruby fast asleep with their carer. The woman in the red dress had finished the night by tending to the children while Rosie and Larry had a few more dances to the sound of the resident band – plus a few 'classical' extra players letting their hair down too.

"I'll leave you two alone now with your family. It was a pleasure to have met you both and to have shared the day with you. I won't forget it. Ruby has gone all out for you and yet she wants to remain in the background. She says it is your day and not hers," whispered Tian as she walked towards the door.

They looked back towards little Ruby, fast asleep in her own bed, clutching her new toy rabbit. Miraculously, the baby was still fast asleep too. Tian knocked on Ruby's door and was greeted with a smile as she was let into her room.

"Thanks Tian for all your help today. You're certainly very versatile and so completely organised on the safety side that I was able to concentrate on the event."

"No Ruby. You are the one who set all these special actions into motion and saw them through to their end. I've never seen so many happy people who have come to together after so much bad history. We'll have to call you Mother Theresa."

Ruby looked at Tian who was beginning to think of Ruby's own 'coming together' which had now turned into a break up.

"It was better to find out now rather than much later when the memories and good times would have made it harder," said Tian quietly.

"Oh, I'm over it already Tian . . . shocked and disappointed but actually I'm glad to see the back of him. The realisation of what he's done has completely overtaken the feelings that I had for him. Once a cheater, always a cheater in my books," replied Ruby sternly.

Tian gave her a hug to whisper her goodbye.

"I have to go back to London now, so I'll say goodnight. I'll see you at your graduation. What a brilliant project to present to the assessors."

"Thanks Tian. I'm really happy that everything worked out well for Rosie and her family. Goodnight."

Tian left the room, closing the door behind her. Ruby looked at the king size bed, then at the bar fridge. Now was the time for a whiskey and coke and a couple of bars of fudge before watching one of the in-house movies on the TV.

"It's time to move on Miss Ruby. Nothing is gained by moping around and feeling sorry for yourself. You are far better than that."

And with that . . . she settled in to watch the movie.

# The Graduate

R uby returned to Redmond Place, noticing that Andrew's red Jaguar was not there. There was an envelope stuck to the front wall of her car bay. She opened it roughly.

Yes, it was from Andrew explaining that he had made a huge mistake, blaming his drinking. He vowed to change his ways, hoping that she would eventually forgive him for ruining their friendship, but realised that their budding relationship was at an end. He said he was sorry so many times and that if she ever wanted to speak to him again, he would be thankful. He went on to say that he was going away for a few weeks to sort himself out.

Ruby thought about Andrew's behaviour during their brief encounter, then about Eric and his unwavering friendship and love. She crumpled up the letter and put it in her bag.

There are no second chances when love is stabbed in the heart by a cheater. Love is a rare enough event requiring trust, fidelity and commitment. The very least she could do was to exchange parking spots with one of the other tenants or ignore

Andrew and his latent conscience, for there was definitely no way that she was going to leave her new home.

She turned her attention to the graduation ceremony at Vauxhall Cross scheduled for her return. She had one afternoon and the evening to prepare her final report and include all the photos to show that her planned interventions into Rosie's life had all been positive – for Rosie and also for her.

Entering her unit, she could still sense the moment she had succumbed to Andrew's advances, wondering if it was his typical modus operandi, to act naive and then pounce on his prey. She got the letter out of her bag and put it through the shredder before relaxing with a drink in front of her computer. The tick boxes on the questionnaire were completed and the body of the report formatted, ready for her project story to be realised in print for the first time.

She stared at the first format heading, 'What do you have planned?' and proceeded to type up her report. It took about four hours to set everything so that it flowed naturally and highlighted how Ruby and Rosie had now become firm friends.

What a story it was. Even a section on how Tian had saved her life from the very person that her classmates had sent to watch over her. A spy sent to report on what she was doing to complete her assignment . . . and to kill her.

Tian called Ruby at 10pm to see if she was still up. Ruby was still deciding what to wear for the morning graduation ceremony. She was in a bit of a panic.

> "Hi Tian, how's everything? I've just finished my report and getting ready for tomorrow. There are clothes everywhere."

> "Remember that it's still a work do Ruby. A business outfit would be preferable. Just checking that all's well with you and to ask if you want picking up tomorrow at say eight o'clock? It'll save you the worry of finding a

parking spot and give you time to relax before presenting your report to class."

Ruby was more relaxed. Someone had decided for her.

"Great Tian, you've helped me make my choice for wearing my blue suit and yes, I would love for you to pick me up at eight."

There was a short silence.

"Seen anything of that Andrew at all? Everything fine with you, about staying there? I mean he is a complete jerk . . . right?" said Tian casually.

"Yes, don't worry about me Tian. I've learnt that no one compares to my Eric. This Andrew thing was just an impulsive . . . whatever . . . and it was mainly from missing Eric. I will not be rushing into anything for a while. It's hard to be alone when you have just lost someone so very close."

"Not your fault. Remember that. It could have been the real thing, but you were very unlucky. Like with my Ilya, you have to let go of the past sometime. Whether you meet someone tomorrow or in a year or never again with the same qualities as the one you have lost . . . time has no part to play when it comes to finding love," replied Tian quietly.

"Do you miss him too Tian, your Ilya?"

"Every hour of every day, I miss him so very much, but I tell myself he is always there in my memories should I want to feel his love. You can do the same with Eric. They were the best Ruby. We were very lucky to have known such love."

"Yes . . . I know you're right . . . See you tomorrow then Tian."

"Bye Ruby. Eight o'clock outside the front."

With the day over, Ruby could at last have a good night's sleep. The report was finished. Andrew was finished. Her wine was finished.

The activities surrounding the double agents and her family's safety as well as the pressure of completing her graduation project had been relentless. Now, calm had once again come into her life.

Morning started with the alarm sounding at six o'clock. Ruby stretched out in her bed, sat up briskly and flopped back again. It was going to be a long day. After a quick shower and change for work it was time for breakfast. Ruby looked at her fridge and wrinkled up her nose.

"No time for that this morning," she said to herself, patting her tummy to check her tunic was not too tight.

A rummage around the pantry produced some energy drinks made from soy and milk. She downed three of them, thinking that she may as well have had a proper breakfast cereal after all.

Ten to eight came too quickly as she glanced through her report printout. She took a USB stick and the print version with her down the lift to the front of the building. Of course, Tian was sitting there in her car, eyes glued to the entrance through a half-open window, with phone in hand ready for calling Ruby at exactly eight o'clock if she hadn't shown.

"Good morning Tian. Prompt as usual as see?"

"Good morning Ruby. A time set is a time well met, as my father used to say. I now always plan to the exact minute and annoy people all the time, so no one can say I'm too early or too late," she said with a slight smile.

Ruby laughed and climbed into the front seat, throwing her sling-bag onto the back seat.

"I wonder who my assessor will be. I hope it's not Josh Camplin that used to shout at me in gym for kicking that Jeffrey guy who kept mauling me all the time when he was supposed to be attacking me. He's the one with the limp," said Ruby sternly.

Tian laughed as she imagined Ruby's impulsive signature defence taking down a burly male recruit.

"You have probably seen your assessor around from time to time Ruby. I hear that the other recruits think this particular assessor is quite particular . . . so you must act confident and project your voice. Your report is obviously very good. Make sure people can hear about it. Oh, and did you know that 'C' will be there as well? He loves to see the trained recruits at their graduation and can sometimes make it known who he wants to be given accelerated processing."

"Wow, now you have me worried. Although I stand by my results and my report," said Ruby with confidence.

"You'll be just fine. Just don't kick anybody."

Tian had her own car parking space which made it easier to head straight for the front entrance. The next stage was to reach the fourth floor down and not a lift to be seen.

"They believe in physical exercise here Ruby and the logistics of having problems with a lift . . . should trouble arrive here, which is highly unlikely," said Tian watching Ruby's strained face at the thought of walking instead of riding.

"It's like an ant colony in here," she replied as Tian stopped.

"And here we are, Room Delta Four M. Let's join the party."

As the door opened to the auditorium, Ruby could see twenty or so smiling eager faces looking at her from the front row seats. There was a bit of talking going on which quickly stopped when they saw Tian, who had stopped to call 'C' on her lapel communicator.

> "Good morning everyone, please be seated and stand when 'C' enters the room. You all of course know Ruby Peters who will be presenting her project to us all . . . and as your final project assessor . . . I can tell you that this particular project is not to be missed," said Tian avoiding Ruby's incredulous stare.

One of the students directed Ruby to her seat, which allowed easy access to the podium. Ruby swallowed and took a deep breath. She had no time to talk with any of her friends because 'C' was following right behind her. As she just about to sit down, everybody else stood up to attention. "C" looked around the room, then at Tian and finally at Ruby.

> "Right then, let's get this dissertation and discussion on the road. Over to you Tian."

Tian smiled at him and turned towards Ruby.

> "Thank you 'C' for attending our turnout today. Ruby Peters is the last of our students to graduate from this class and as required, the floor is now open for her to present her final project, followed by a short question time. If you will, please Ruby. The stage is all yours," said Tian, showing Ruby to the podium with that familiar proud look.

Ruby strode out to the centre of the room and up the steps to the podium. She turned around. A feeling of pride and belonging swelled within her. She took her time. She looked at each of the graduates, Tian, 'C' and down to her notes. She looked up again and put her notes to one side.

"Thank you 'C', Tian . . . my assessor . . . my classmates
and future operational team members. This day has
taken so long to arrive and yet paradoxically . . . it has
arrived as if driven by a wild storm."

Everyone was hoping for her not to become too emotional
and awkward in her treatment of the sequence of events in her
personal life. Ruby continued with a tone of survival.

"As you may know, I have been through rather a lot in
my time with you as a recruit, in my personal life . . .
with family, friends and people very, very close to me . .
. but . . . but I will not be speaking about that today. For
today, I want to tell you all about my project and the
person I hated most at my school. 'Blizzard Face' is the
girl who I used to stare-out and try to destroy by calling
her names and standing over her as she did with me."

The audience was laughing and Ruby was on her way.

"This project taught me a very important lesson, and I
think that is why we are given it to understand . . . that
someone who you hate and who then hates you back,
can go on to become that someone who means the
world to you. For, by doing something good for their
situation and in parallel doing good for the sake of
helping someone without them knowing until later . . .
your perception of people as good, bad or indifferent
will be open for challenge. It is not the first time this
has been realised. The ancient saying of 'bringing your
enemies near to your heart' has certainly been proven to
me, by what has occurred over the last few weeks.
Through this project, we have learnt to actually make
them friends since those ancient days, where they
generally used to poison them. Now I present my
analysis of the project."

For the next thirty minutes, Ruby explained what she had set out to do, to make Rosie Winters life better by helping her solve some problems that seemed insurmountable to her.

The final part of this 'gift' was to give her a wedding that she would not forget, as well as bringing all of the outcast family members together and showing herself to be the friend that she did not know was there all the time.

The end of her speech was a run-down of the positive aspects of what she had done.

> "This project has brought together many people, but I insist that majority of the credit should go to the participants who were only too eager to grasp the concept of this idea. I was purely the director of a film that only needed to be realised by its writers, actors, set designers and you . . . the audience.

> Foremost, we have Rosie and me who have reconciled our differences and totally unknown to me at the time . . . had already named her own daughter Ruby after me, because she thought we could have been friends. Who would have picked that for starters?

> Then there is Rosie and her step-father along with her mother. They were slowly healing their differences because they recognised the innocence of Rosie's children within their relationship. Rosie's husband Larry now has a cohesive loving family to live with . . . and he has now reconciled with his own father who has eagerly joined the extended family.

> To make amends for Rosie's father, who left the family when she was just six years old, he has now written to her with what I hear is the start of a renewed friendship.

> As a further note to that, I will be examining the case of Rosie's dad in which I think at this stage, it does look as

though he was framed for his crime. The police are re-examining the evidence.

Finally, I put my relationship with Rosie as my first bit of good news in a while. Now, I have my relationship with this new extended family, which is my second bit of great news. There is also the practical experience I've gained in using interview techniques and covert photography in gaining the evidence.

On a sad note and with a lesson to be learned by everyone . . . I regret the death of Alan Barker who was one of us . . . and yet chose to follow the same pathway as the other traitors, all of them now eliminated from our organisation.

It would seem that I have escaped death by the simple distance of night over day. Some may have known his good side and maybe his project would have been super exciting. However, watching and studying my demise with photos would not have made for very good reading for me . . . if he was standing here instead of me. Thank you everyone. Are there any questions?"

There was a huge round of applause and Tian went up to shake her hand.

"I may have to pass you Miss Peters after all," joked Tian.

"I might have known you would figure somewhere in all this Tian. You are my lifeline and closest friend and are like a mentor . . . just like Roger Davis," Ruby whispered.

The audience loved her performance and after the applause quietened down, two people raised their hands to ask questions.

"Ruby, can you tell me how on earth you have remained so calm and grounded after all the events in your life since leaving school? I mean, you seem to be totally indestructible," asked Ken Smithurst before sitting down again.

Ruby looked at him with a grin on her face.

"It is not so much what happened to me and the ones I wanted to protect so much Ken, but having the right people around me at the time. As you know, my Eric was a real hero . . . in that he saved my life on a few occasions . . . and Tian, your assessor and her dear friend Ilya Kasparov . . . and my parents and the Legionnaires . . . I could name quite a few. But to answer your question . . . and to quote my very first mentor in this precarious industry, 'There's no such thing as coincidence. What we have is contrivance and a well-made plan . . . and therefore an audit trail for us to unlock the past and discover their weaknesses" . . . so know your enemy.' So all I can say is that we must be wary of things that look and feel contrived."

Ken stood up again.

"And who was that Ruby? Who was your mentor?"

Ruby looked at Tian and then glanced towards an uncomfortable looking 'C'.

"His name was Roger Davis and is buried not fifteen miles from here. He was the one who recruited me . . . and Eric. He died protecting my life. He should be the one standing here today instead of me."

Another student rose from her seat to break the awkwardness of the moment.

"Hi Ruby, I'm Jennifer Soames. We did some earlier work together if you remember."

"Yes I remember you Jenni, what do you want to know?"

Jennifer looked a bit edgy and looked at 'C' sideways before asking her the question.

> "Well Ruby, for the benefit of us students . . . I mean graduates . . . can you tell me what it feels like to survive just one of the many encounters where you could have lost your life. I mean, did you ever think to yourself that the cost was far too high and that you should just get out of the whole thing?"

It was obvious that the class had been thinking the same thing and had been dwelling on that for quite a while on hearing of Ruby's appalling string of misadventures and personal loss of so many close friends, in some of the most gruesome ways.

Ruby did not need much time to think.

> "We are all in this together Jenni and it is near impossible to contemplate leaving the service because of what's happened, otherwise it would all have been for nothing. Then there's my view that if we didn't stop these dangerous people who have no moral code or regret for what they do, then my family and your families are all at risk of being injured or even murdered by being in the wrong place, a miscalculation, a wrong factual error or what have you . . . someone has to stop them before it happens. That's what we have been trained to do. I didn't have that training earlier on. Things may have been much different if I had been trained. You actually get to a point where you no longer get hurt. I mean you still have your emotions, but the thought of harm and death becomes less fearful because there are more important things to consider."

The class cheered her on as 'C' approached the podium, waving for Ruby to sit down. He looked relieved it was over.

"Thank you Ruby for a most interesting and enlightening insight into your project and how you have changed lives through your project and much more besides. We all so much appreciate your honesty and sincerity. I have not heard in all my years, such a factual and yet touching account of a new graduate's experience after completing their final project. I also note with much sadness and regret, the passing of so many of our colleagues and that of your mentor Roger Davis, your boyfriend Eric Johnson and former Russian agent Ilya Kasparov. Our thoughts go out to their friends and families. Now, to finish on a happier note, it is my duty and most importantly my pleasure to announce that you have all completed the requirements of your graduation with success and I am most happy about presenting the graduation trophy to graduate Grade Three . . . Ruby Peters for her outstanding work and call to duty, in the face of great odds, and at such a young age."

"Grade Three!" mouthed Ruby.

The applause was overwhelming and seemed to contradict the number of people in the audience until she looked up towards the balcony seats at the back of the auditorium.

Standing up and waving were her mum and dad, Eric's family, Rosie and her family, ten ex-legionnaires . . . and one Mister Tan, the Chinese negotiator . . . Tian's father.

"Ruby, please come up to the front to collect your trophy and accreditation," beckoned 'C'.

The sight of Ruby collecting her trophy and thanking everyone was a remarkable sight. The small gathering was given a few minutes to combine and socialise before some food was brought in. The strict guideline was that they all had to be away within the hour allocated. Towards the end, 'C' had a quiet word with Ruby.

"I'm sorry to bring up business on the very day that you celebrate becoming an FIO, grade three no less . . . but I have some important things to ask you Ruby. As I said previously, you will be working directly with me under the supervision of Tian."

Ruby looked a bit surprised at this new business talk on her graduation day and just nodded.

"Your Eric was the best code breaker that we never had. His quick assessment of Roger's letter, leading to the diamond engraving was second to none. Our people were stumped, as you know. Then the coding on the engraving was another breakthrough in finding our moles . . . although you could say they found us in most cases. Now I know that you sold the diamonds to give some of the money to your parents and friends . . . but we have no account of the original inscriptions that were on those diamonds. Tell me, do you still have that diamond for us to . . . check, Ruby?"

Ruby was surprised that they had not asked for it earlier. She knew that they had a copy of Roger Davis's letter and Eric's superb deconstruction of its coding. But why ask now, after all the people on her list which was available to MI6 through her . . . were in fact locked away or dead.

"Well, first off, I had the diamond with the inscription broken down into smaller pieces to erase the information and to make it easier to sell as smaller lots. The original copy of the list is hidden away, with the intention of handing it in once I graduated, as part of the evidence for the conviction of the double-agents, and . . ."

She was interrupted by the irritated 'C'.

"And . . . was there anything else inscribed on the diamond?"

"No, just what you have already seen which match the names of the moles, except in code."

"And what about the letter from Roger Davis . . . was there anything else that Eric could see in the drawings and other details . . . words, numbers?"

"Why do you ask? Was there something that you were particularly looking for?"

'C' looked uncomfortable again.

"No, not really . . . but we thought that Roger may have had a secret location for some of his other papers and . . . ideas and all that. You know . . . his glory box of past cases and leads and that sort of thing. We never found a will or anything to do about his assets at all at his various hiding places."

"Well, you have the letter yourself. I'm surprised GCHQ can't work out any other details now that it has been fully explained by Eric's analysis. You know if hadn't been for Eric, your MI6 could still have Peter Richards, Geoffrey Tunsdon and Henry Roberts working alongside you. I can't imagine how there could there be anything else?" said Ruby suspiciously.

She had not really looked at the letter in great detail, relying on Eric's translation of the coding.

"Oh quite, yes, I'm sure that there is nothing else untoward on that letter . . . or was inscribed on that now destroyed diamond perhaps?"

He looked at her as if she had destroyed the diamond just to thwart the investigation, but then he was not sure about that.

The rest of the day for Ruby was filled with celebration and close family talk, with everyone catching up and sharing their latest news. Mum and dad were heading back to Liverpool and Milly and Robbie were looking at buying into a new hotel in

Cornwall. Larry had been offered an interview at GCHQ. The bombshell of the evening was when Larry proposed a toast to Ruby and then lingered on his final words.

> "I want to thank Ruby for all that she has done for everyone sitting here tonight. She has brought great joy and united together our families in a way that I think is like magic . . . and while we are at it . . . I want you all to raise your glasses to both Ruby and Rosie . . . and to share our news that Rosie expecting her third baby."

There was chaos within the group as well-oiled participants chinked their glasses together amid cheers and much shouting.

Ruby went home alone as her parents were staying in a hotel overnight put up by the 'company'. She was exhilarated and tired and felt quite happy about the turning point in her turbulent life. One thing bothered her. She had the notes for the inscription on that diamond and also the letter from Roger Davis. She knew the inscription did not contain any more information, as the names had been decoded, with nothing left over.

She went over to her secret stash in the wall cavity that she had made in the kitchen near the air extractor over the cooker. Taking it to the armchair under the stronger reading light in the room, she looked at it closely for the first time.

Now that Eric had decoded it, she could easily make out the six words that defined the properties of a diamond along with the words 'Lazier' for laser and 'Bug' which Eric had made into carat based on Bugs Bunny. The two triangles showed a coming together to make a diamond shape and the K2R4F8 represented the laser frequency 248 from a KRF laser, the same one used for etching diamonds by de Beers.

But wait . . . what was that extra piece of information in the form of 'Recall' and 'Switch' on one side of the diagram.

She thought about it for about an hour. All sorts of ideas came to mind but none that made any sense. Then she remembered 'C' telling her that Davis may have had a private stash of information, hidden away from prying eyes.

She remembered him playing games with her and the diamonds that day at the Morpeth Arms, taking her attention away while he opened up the box to switch one of the diamonds before slipping in a badge under the tray of diamonds . . . all without her noticing. It was a switch or sleight of hand. She jumped up excitedly and ran to the bedroom.

> "Remember Ruby. Switch is like Swiss . . . Swiss. It's on the badge. Oh my god, the My6 badge that he gave me," she murmured remembering Davis's words.

Rummaging through her jewellery box, she found the badge and quickly looked at it. The light was too dim. She raced back to the lounge and drew it closer to the lamp. There was a number on the back, but that was all. Nothing else anywhere and nothing would come apart. She checked the number again and began thinking like Eric would have done, not by logic but by sheer intuition and trial and error.

The serial number consisted of three parts:

FY1-234D-49275

Ruby looked up the postcodes and found that FY1 was the postcode for Blackpool. Sure, he had always talked about going there for studying the wider mix of people who visited during the summer, with the intention of studying their characteristics.

Roger was very methodical in his attempt to get accents and body language correct for his creative undercover work. He would not only be able to tell where someone was from, but he could also act out the same character by voice on the phone or by mannerism on the job . . . combined with suitable clothing and attitude to match the job.

Ruby looked at the other numbers and immediately knew she had cracked it. It was so clear now that an inner voice had virtually replaced the numbers with an image. Roger Davis had a post office box or railway station private box 234D which uses the PIN 49275. She had to go there. She was meant to retrieve his things and possibly act on it.

Ruby started thinking about Eric again. How wonderful but annoying it would have been to follow through with this new information, with him constantly informing her that his method of analysis had won the day. She smiled at his intuitive ways.

That was the biggest reason she thought she hated him at school – he was just too intuitive and casually smart -but usually right. Ruby's new adventure under the very eyes of MI6 had already started.

She suddenly thought of another idea. Quickly she raced to her computer and looked up 'Swiss Blackpool'. The answer revealed the final piece to the cryptic jigsaw.

"Swiss Bus Company – Blackpool. We can store your valuables for you – private boxes available now. Choose a tour today."

Ruby had a quiet moment in all the excitement.

"You have even got me to think differently . . . you little rascal. It is as if I am looking through the prism of a sparkling diamond with each glint of light revealing the fractured thoughts running wildly at random into my mind's eye. Thank you Eric . . . or rather my 'Diamond for a Ruby'."

# The Legacy

Ruby got up bright and early on Saturday morning with clear intentions. She had formulated a plan.

She had prepared the day before and was excited about travelling 'undercover' from her own people, away from the prying eyes that she knew were waiting for her next move . . . to retrieve the expected stash that Davis had left behind in anticipation of his unexpected but foreseeable death. It was part of his character to prepare meticulously for such an event, even to the point of choosing Ruby and Eric to follow his cryptic clues to reach his final resting place far beyond the grave.

A young woman in jeans, jacket and flat running shoes emerged from the back of the Redmond Place unit block at five o'clock, bounding effortlessly over the back wall into the street behind her own, with a sling bag over her shoulder. She had already sprayed the security camera with a dark ice powder that would thaw and leave no remains after ten minutes.

She tied her hair up tight into a ponytail. She was wearing gloves. All her clothes were bought new the day before to ensure that they had not been tagged. She had to outperform Tian, who would definitely have been ordered to follow her.

Walking a good mile away from her home, she flagged down a roaming taxi, directing it to a busy shopping district and paying the driver by cash. Mingling amongst the early shoppers, she stopped for a coffee and sandwiches, watching for any sign of a tail. Someone like Tian would be very stealthy and would be hard to spot amongst the public surroundings.

Ruby put on her dark glasses now that it was light and went through to the back of the shop where the toilets were located, disappearing into the alleyway, walking quickly to a string of taxis sitting on a rank, choosing the first one. She directed the driver to the British Museum.

She paid in cash and ran into the museum, walking briskly to the second exit point, now wearing a grey raincoat, where an old Transit Van was waiting for her, as arranged the previous day using her new cover name of Katarina Davidoff. She had paid for the white van in cash from a most disreputable car yard recommended by Davis in one of his brief talks with her. Its windows had a medium tint, as Davis would have liked.

Ruby put on her black beret after letting her hair fall loose, which she much preferred. She smiled knowing she was free.

With a quick look in her rear vision mirror and then slowly swivelling the side mirrors around to make sure she was not under observation, she took a deep breath and drove off towards the interchange for the M40 motorway, which joins the M6 to Blackpool.

She had not booked a hotel, as one full day away would be enough to determine if her hunch had been correct and she would be back in London by ten o'clock. It would be dark enough to scale the back wall of her building again.

It had been a long time since Ruby felt so free and relaxed and with the window half-open, singing her 'Ruby Max' chorus, she headed off towards the Fylde Coast. The van was not the quietest vehicle on the road but it did the job and was really the ideal vehicle for blending in with all the trucks and commercial vehicles that passed her by.

When she reached Preston on the boundary to the Fylde Coast, it was not long before the iron beacon, known as the 'tower' to locals came into view. Everything else was flat and the main road seemed to be so smooth and neat as it wound its way into the ring road around Blackpool.

Ruby looked for the street where the Swiss Bus Company operated. The advert mentioned that there was a service to London at two o'clock that afternoon which appealed to her.

Turning into Hornby Road near the centre of town, she did not have to look very far for the company depot. A huge tourist bus had just arrived in front of their small office, where two billboards with tacky paintings of the Swiss Alps featuring a little man with moustache, alpine hat and a friendly cow appeared to welcome even the most economically disadvantaged passengers to its doors.

Ruby parked the van around the corner and looked back at it with regret whilst removing her gloves. She was beginning to like the dented van, which she had already named 'Boris' to suit her disguise.

"Good morning, and what can I do for you today? Are you wanting our special mystery tour that starts in fifteen minutes or something further afield?" started the friendly man in a uniform that looked too closely like the little man on the signage.

"Good morning. I want to book the two o'clock bus to London this afternoon . . . but first I have this private box number, which I think is located here. My friend organised it about three years ago but he is now unable to come here . . . he has problems with his feet. Do you have such boxes here?" asked Ruby with great empathy for the man's obvious enthusiasm.

The man looked at the number and then carefully at Ruby.

"So he is having trouble walking is he, that little Irish scallywag. Yes, I know him love. Used to come here every summer for a day or two to take in the air he said. He always left me a big tip for looking after his stuff and then when he didn't show I thought that he may have travelled overseas like he said he was going to. He's a funny guy, that old Jimmy."

"Yes, James was a right card alright. So, do you have his stuff? I have the security code to open up what looks like a sealed box maybe?" asked Ruby casually.

The man looked her up and down again and nodded his head.

"Aye it's here alright. Just show me some identification love and I'll get the box right now. You will have to open it while I'm here so as I can keep the box, but I'll give you a bag to put everything in. Now then, what's your name then love?"

Ruby had to think fast. She had forgotten already.

"Oh yes, I'm Katarina Davidoff although my friends call me Kata. Here is my driving license. I'll pay you for the bus fare too to secure my ride."

The man looked at her and grinned. It was as if he already knew her in a friendly sort of way. He went away and returned with a box that was about the same size as a shoebox.

"Right then Kata love, use your security code to open the box and I'll look away while you empty the contents into this bag."

Ruby was not taking any chances, as the bag could have been tagged.

"No that's alright. I'll just put everything into my sling bag."

The man wandered to the back of the room where the ticket machine was located as another customer fronted up to make a booking.

Ruby opened the box and without looking at the contents quickly emptied everything into her bag. She then took out her purse and counted out the cash required for her return trip to London. The man took the cash and gave her a ticket. He had that knowing smile again as if he knew what was going on which caused Ruby to feel a chill.

"Make sure you're back here by about one-thirty love. The bus leaves dead on two o'clock . . . not a second later."

Ruby nodded and gave him a hesitant smile as she was leaving. She would find another way back and maybe take her van to the next town with a train station.

She noticed from occasional sideways glances that he was still looking at her with that same smile. She reasoned that if he had wanted to, he could have opened that box himself at any time without anyone knowing. Therefore, she took it as reasonable that this man was either no threat or was stringing her along . . . but she would take precautions anyway.

Ruby had never been to Blackpool. Crowds of people who seemed to be having a fantastic time walked on either side of her as she wondered where to go, to be alone with her treasures.

She thought about going to the sandy beach and hiring a deck chair or maybe walking along one of the three piers in the holiday town to find an empty seat . . . or maybe into the tower itself via the aquarium and up high in the lift to the top.

She was becoming indecisive again.

Her bus ticket had advertising on the back, which showed that Stanley Park was going to host a gala bagpipe event later in the year.

> "The park sounds just nice and private for my thoughts," she whispered to herself.

After conducting various manoeuvres to throw off any attempt at tailing her, she emerged out of souvenir shop with a few 'attachments' to make her blend in with the crowd.

It was a warm day as she wandered slowly down to Stanley Park and once inside found a nice cafe that served coffee and her favourite . . . delicious vanilla slices. There was a nice table near the window overlooking a large rose garden. Ruby sat down and slowly removed various items from her bag, which opened at the top to expose its entire contents.

There was a thick white envelope, three passports, a wad of cash, foreign credit cards, a photo album and a set of car keys.

Ruby took another deep breath and sighed, knowing that Roger Davis had planned this day a long time ago, realising that he would never get to share it with her. She resisted the urge to cry and steeled herself for what could be in the envelope.

She opened it carefully as the contents were bulging, filling out the volume to breaking point. There was a letter, a bundle of legal documents, a bank account summary and a photo of him smiling back at her with a wink.

She started to read the letter:

> 'Congratulations Ruby and Eric on getting thus far. I knew you would of course. Oh and say hello to Jacko from me. He is the one in the funny outfit behind the counter at Swiss. I told him you would come one day, probably with some outlandish name – especially that Eric of yours. He could never resist going over the top. Diamond indeed!

You can trust Jacko with your life. I have on numerous occasions. Alas, but this time I am not in a position to do that myself – because you are here and I am obviously not. Life sucks sometimes love.

I will keep this brief. I want you both to do what you will with the list of double agents etched on the diamond that I switched when you were preoccupied with that badge. The people named must be shut down. Again, only trust 'C' and Tian as by now you will know that Tian was working with me – she is just the best Ruby.

Anyway, don't worry about me too much. I had a good innings so far and I want you to accept my belongings as a statement of how I valued your very essence of what I love about life.

So, you will find my old passport which I used to get away when times were tough. There are two passports for you and Eric to use in the same way. While I am still breathing the Blackpool air, I will keep updating the photos of you both – albeit with a touch of age. You will like the photo album – all taken when you were not looking.

There is a property in Queensland Australia and a boat in a marina in Hobart Tasmania for you to hide out or maybe stay there to live out your days in peace and quiet. And a bank account with sufficient funds to retire at any age – you lucky kids!

The keys are for my car situated in Australia. The details are in the paperwork enclosed.

I want to apologise for hiring you both when underage and for all the stress and troubles I've caused you and your families.

However, you turned out to be worthy of such duties and I thank you for all your help and friendship.

One last thing! Please take my ashes and spread them from Mount Wellington in Hobart, to ride the roaring forties to god knows where. I hate that bloody cemetery where they bury us unfortunates. It's full of dead people!

Much love from one who cared so much for you. I don't know what either of you will be doing but I expect that you will both be the best at what you do. Hope you stay together forever.

Thank Tian for me as well. NO, there is nothing here for her . . . she is able to look after herself and you two.

Goodbye Ruby and Eric (alias Scarlett and Diamond),

Signed: Roger Davis (alias everyone that I borrowed from, for my life's play)'

S he thumbed through the photo album. The photos showed them in various locations . . . they looked innocent and raw. Some snaps of her made her realise just how naive she had been. The final photo was of Ruby taking a shower with the caption:

'Must have one of these in my next life !!!'

"You cheeky bugger," she gasped, closing up the book quickly.

Ruby looked out at the rose garden as tears began rolling down her warm cheeks. She was all alone in a holiday town brimming with happy people on holiday.

"You alright love?"

The waitress had brought her a huge vanilla slice and was concerned about her apparent sadness. Ruby looked up at her, wiping her eyes and smiling thankfully.

> "Yes I'm fine thank you. Just a sad letter from an old friend who has written some beautiful words for me," replied Ruby.

The waitress smiled at her and placed her flat white coffee on the table. The cream had a face on it with a wide smile.

> "A friend is both hard to find and even harder to lose my dear."

Ruby put the letter back in her bag and looked through the passports. She was surprised.

Roger's passport had the name Ben E. Volante. Ruby laughed at her mentor's cryptic humour. The next passport showed her dear Eric, but the name was definitely Damon Spier and his photo had been photoshopped to show him with grey touches and a moustache to give him some age. Ruby was looking at what Eric may have looked like at age thirty. She paused to take a deep breath to stop more tears.

Her own passport showed a similarly aged woman with shorter blond hair, leaving Ruby amazed at how good it looked on her. Then she saw her name . . . Scarlett Angel.

> "Now really Roger, who would ever believe that was real?"

Then she looked at the profession . . . 'Actress and Author'.

Shaking her head, Ruby put the passports away and reached for the legal documents. There was a house in Queensland on ten acres of land just outside of Brisbane. The title deeds were in her name. Then there was paperwork and a marina contract for a permanent berth just north of Hobart, for a forty foot yacht complete with an annual maintenance contract. It was a ketch, whatever that was.

Finally, there were the registration papers for a car . . . a Mercedes four-wheel drive and an ongoing contract for an office, in the city of Brisbane itself . . . with a business name set up for 'Gem International'.

Ruby was cheering up now that the initial shock had passed. Her newfound freedom was just a step away whenever she needed it. She looked around the cafe and bundled up everything into her bag before waving and saying goodbye to the waitress.

She was originally going to forfeit her bus ticket and catch the train but had now decided to call in to see Jacko to thank him for keeping Roger's papers safe from the authorities.

He was waiting for her as she arrived to board the bus.

> "So, it is Jacko isn't it? Thank you for looking after Roger's things. He wrote in his letter that you were the only one he could trust. That means a lot to me."

> "Well, and may I say Ruby that you are as lovely as he kept telling me, I finally get to meet you in person. But, where's that young 'Eric the diamond' then?" he said quietly with a smile.

Ruby started to say something, anything . . . but she broke down and sobbed. Jacko walked over to her and put his arm around her.

> "I'm so sorry love. I think I know what may have happened and I am so very sorry for you. You know you can always come back here at any time and I'll see to it that you have anything you want . . . no questions asked. I owe it to Roger. I now know why he has been keeping away these last years. He did expect it one day you know."

Ruby looked up at him and thanked him with a nod of her head before boarding the bus, which had thundered into life.

As the bus left for London, Ruby waved goodbye to Jacko who was looking rather sad now, realising that both Roger Davis and young Eric had no longer any way of seeing how Ruby was coping so well with her overwhelming grief.

But they would be proud he reckoned . . . that's for sure.

About the author:

Stefan Andrew Nicholson, MA (Swinburne) has had a multiple career in Science and Technology with an unstoppable undercurrent to author books and compose music. He is the author of eleven books which include three novels, a four-part short story book, poetry and an invented international symbol language called "Symbolic Art Notation".

He has also composed more than fifty musical compositions producing a DVD "Pictures of Life" with twenty of them recorded on seventeen tracks for full orchestra and band. He is a member of the Australian Society of Authors, a Fellow of the Institute of Scientific and Technical Communicators and has spent fifteen years as a Technical Writer and Multi-Media designer.

He lives in Hobart, Tasmania on his boat "Nickinoff" in the Prince of Wales Bay Marina.